DESPERATE JOURNEYS

SAISNATH BAIJOO

Order this book online at www.trafford.com
or email orders@trafford.com

Most Trafford titles are also available at major online book retailers.

Print information available on the last page.

ISBN: 978-1-4907-8764-0 (sc)
ISBN: 978-1-4907-8765-7 (hc)
ISBN: 978-1-4907-8773-2 (e)

Library of Congress Control Number: 2018936177

Trafford rev. 04/25/2018

www.trafford.com
North America & international
toll-free: 1 888 232 4444 (USA & Canada)
fax: 812 355 4082

CONTENTS

Foreword vii

Chapter One: Our Normadic Instinct 1
Chapter Two: Our Journey Begins With One Step 19
Chapter Three: The Cuban Migration: Is the
                    Grass Greener on the Other Side? 34
Chapter Four: A Clash Of Cultures: East Meets
                    The West 70
Chapter Five: A Journey Into the Afterlife: Is it
                    Real? 118
Chapter Six: A Journey Into Incurable Diseases 141
Chapter Seven: A Journey Not by Choice 164
Chapter Eight: Enjoy Your Journey 179

E very journey starts with one step. A desperate journey starts with several frenetic steps in no logical direction. A desperate journey is comparable to a drowning man hanging on to straws to prevent his inevitable demise. Since the dawn of mankind, by instinct or to survive perilous times, primitive man followed the food trail. When resources were dwindling, their leaders directed their people desperate search of more fertile grounds.

Primitive men were generally nomadic. They did not respect borders. Therefore, no country can boast with confidence that their people are of truly a single pure race. As my book progresses, there will be sufficient evidence to prove my statements.

Wars were very frequent. It was the survival of the strongest and most aggressive tribes. The captured masses were massacred or enslaved at the whims and fancies of their captors. The victors determined their fate. The women were raped, were married, or became slaves, leading to the crossbreeding of races. The conquerors determined what name, culture, and religion the vanquished were given. Their enslaved ones were given a simple choice of either to adapt or to die.

An example of this was when the Europeans arrived to America; they annihilated the Native Americans in the good name of Christianity and greediness. A culture that lived generally in peace for centuries was decimated in a short time. Sadly, the Native Americans initially welcomed the Europeans with open arms. Even today, the Sioux Tribe of Dakota are fighting an uphill battle to prevent an oil pipeline from polluting their sacred ancestral lands. Remember, they were the original settlers in America, many centuries before the Europeans invaded their lands.

Meanwhile, on the other side of the globe, similar atrocities were a common occurrence. I quote from quora.com, "About 90 percent of Muslims and 95 percent of Christians who reside in India, Pakistan, Sri Lanka, Bangladesh, Myanmar, Afghanistan, and Nepal were all ancestral Hindus. They were all converted to Islam either by deadly brute force or by enticing them to a better way of life. The same pattern occurred with Christianity in India."

Francois Gautier, in his book *Rewriting Indian History* (1996), wrote, "The massacres perpetuated by Muslims in India are unparalleled in history, bigger than the Holocaust of the Jews by the Nazis; or the massacre of the Armenians by the Turks; more extensive even than the slaughter of the South American native population by the invading Spanish and Portuguese."

In the dangerous legacy of Genghis Khan's Mongol Empire, it is a fact that sixteen million individuals alive today still carry his Y chromosome. He lived a thousand years ago, yet one out of every two hundred men still possesses his genes. As the murderous victor boastfully said, "The greatest joy for a man is to defeat his enemies, to drive them before him, to take from them all they possess, to see those they love in tears, to ride their horses, and to hold their wives and daughters in his arms."

Supremacy and total domination are the inevitable heartbreak of all wars. The first humans are believed to have left Africa via the Arabian coast and through India before reaching Indonesia and New Guinea and, finally, over an ancient land bridge to Australia more than forty-five thousand years ago. Analysis of DNA samples from Aboriginal people living in the Northern Territories of Australia today shows that they have up to 11 percent of their genetic heritage as Indian.

Man, by nature, always has that brutal and animalistic instinct. He is always yearning to grab hold of his neighbor's wealth because of greed, ambition, hatred, or simple petty jealousy. This book tries to shed light on some fascinating journeys throughout man's existence. The priority of my book is foremost for my readers' enlightenment, inspiration, and enjoyment to your life. My approach is a bit serious yet comical but not boring. Nevertheless, this book has a serious message for the world. Extend that loving hand to help everyone. *Desperate Journeys* are not just traveling from one part of the world to another seeking refuge. My book encompasses journeys that are physical, mental, and spiritual. Together, we will journey into the afterlife.

Presently, countries such as USA, India, and China have successfully sent missions to the planet Mars. Are these desperate journey attempts by world leaders seeking a new and habitable world? We are living in dangerous yet exciting times. Access to any information is at our fingertips through the Internet at any given time. Do you think that modern technology has brought the world closer together? Closer, Yes, but has mankind lost their passion to care for their fellow human beings? Violent videos on social media acquire the most likes. Hatred seems to be more popular amongst families, friends and neighbors. True love, commitment and compassion have taken a back seat. Marriages are not sacred, and love is for convenience. Politicians have capitalized on this weakness to propagate discord among their people. Divide and rule are their motto to stay in power. As an author, I am honestly allergic to long and boring novels. Therefore, it is my utmost and honest intentions to make this novel as realistic, interesting, comical, romantic, inspiring, graphic, griping, and exciting as humanly possible.

CHAPTER ONE

Our Normadic Instinct

I sat slouching in my chair with my feet perched on my desk. My medical office is closed for the moment. However, my mind was preoccupied, contemplating about this journey called life. Why were we placed on this planet? Are we actors in a stage called life? Do we just exist as humans to eat, get fat, accumulate wealth, get old, shrivel away, and eventually die? Sadly, we leave everything behind that we have accumulated. As the good books philosophically say, "From dust we came, and from dust we will return." Is this the sole purpose of mankind's existence—from dust to dust? Do we embark upon another journey after we die? At my striving medical practice, every one of my patients seems to be miserable, sad, or depressed. There are rarely any happy or smiling faces. The nature of the human mind in my limited knowledge is that people are never contented with the little or grand wealth at their disposal. My psychiatric practice is based on this weakness of the human spirit.

My name is Jonathan, your humble author. The sounds of laughter from my patients, staff, and especially from my family truly bring tears of happiness to my eyes. As my loving mother would say, "Laughter and love are extremely contagious. Always pass it on to others. A pleasant smile is free and helps keep your sanity. Contaminate the world with it. Smile." My deceased mother had instilled that idea in my stubborn head. Life's journey is too short. Enjoy the ride. Death and diseases are no respecter of age, wealth, or race. There is no warranty for living or dying so enjoy the journey of a good life while you are still healthy. Get rid of that frown from your face. Remember, you cannot please everyone, so live and let live. A smile releases that pent-up tension. A sincere smile relaxes my mind, body, and spirit. This is not my original story, but it relates to my appropriate values in this book.

The story is told of an old man and his son who were fed up about being judged by others until the following happened to them. An old man, a boy, and their donkey were going far out of town on business. The journey was long and treacherous. On their way, they passed some people who laughed and said, "What a cruel shame that the old man is walking. The old man looks sick and weary. The boy looks healthy but so lazy. He should not be riding." The man and boy overheard their silly comments. They were sad and truly believed their critics were so right. They willingly changed their positions, hoping to please their detractors.

As their long journey continued, they passed some more meddlesome people who sniggered and threw stones at them. They remarked, "What a shame! He makes that weak little boy walk on the dirt road while he relaxes on the poor donkey. The strong old man should be ashamed. He should be punished." Then, they agreed that they both will walk.

Soon they passed more prying people who laughed mockingly. "They are really dumb and definitely stupid. They have a donkey to give them a decent ride, yet these stupid people are walking." Trying to please everyone, they both decided to ride the donkey.

Soon they passed some people who humiliated them by saying, "How awful to put such a load on a poor, weak donkey." The boy and the old man figured that their nosy critics were probably right again. They decided to lift the donkey. The donkey was very heavy. As they crossed the narrow bridge, they lost their grip on the donkey. The poor animal fell into the river and drowned.

The moral of the story is, in life, create your own journey—a journey that comes from the heart and carved to your pathway is your right choice. Walk in your own shoes, and do not be a copycat and walk in other people's shoes. Ignore negative comments that serve to demean your life. Harsh words do not kill, but they cut wounds deep into our hearts. Generally, people are judgmental in a negative way. Your life's journey is unique. Enjoy the ride of life with its many rollercoasters. Here is an appropriate comment with a positive and vibrant quotation from famous American actor, Richard Gere: "None of us are getting out of here alive, so please stop treating yourself like an afterthought. Eat delicious food. Walk in the sunshine. Jump in the ocean. Say the truth that you are carrying in your heart like hidden treasure. Be silly. Be kind. Be weird. There is no time for anything else."

The journey through life is hostile and full of pitfalls. There is no guarantee of success. Failure hides with every journey. It is complex and uncertain beyond a shadow of a doubt. There is no road map for life's difficult journey. There is no GPS to give directions for success. There are a privileged few that are born with that utopic gold spoon in their mouth. However, for most people, success comes through diligent work and literally burning the midnight's oil.

This book examines the journeys of the physical, mental, and spiritual lives of our people on this planet. Recently, there have been countless accounts of mass exodus from the Middle East. It is a fact that every one of us is an immigrant in some footpath of our lives. This book seeks to explore the psyche behind these mass exodus or immigration. What makes people flee desperately from their place of birth, leaving all their earthly and family ties, and then they go like beggars seeking refugee status in other countries? It means starting a new and uncertain life and having to adapt to a different language and a foreign culture. Meaningless wars, murdering dictators, religious fanatics, and communist regimes have aided and abetted in these mass exoduses.

This book will follow refugees throughout the ages to understand their diverse cultures and thought patterns behind their departure from their beloved homeland. Oddly enough, many refugees have fled persecutions from their treasured country where their culture and religious dogma have suppressed their freedom of expression. Sadly, when they settle in their adopted country, they seek to emulate the very barbaric teachings that suppressed them in their country of birth. Mankind has not learned from the deadly blunders of their past generations. Two senseless world wars that decimated millions of people and ruined many prosperous countries have not really influenced our love for wars. We have turned a blind eye to the evils of history. Have we learned from the mistakes of our evil past? No, we have not.

Readers, if we have not learned from the mistakes of past generations, then we will certainly repeat their wrong deeds. The world has not changed. It is the people in this world who behave uncivilized. Mother Nature willingly absorbs the cruelty and pollution administered by mankind to her.

I sincerely believe that anger is a byproduct of fear. This fear boils into hatred and jealousy. Fanatical religious intolerance and racial divide have played major roles to compound this hatred. People quote scriptures to show that their beliefs have the correct version of God's word and try to impose their beliefs on other faiths even through violent means. Has anyone seen the face of God? No not one. Many senseless wars have been fought over differing religious beliefs.

I would like to share a quotation from Emperor Haile Selassie of Ethiopia. He said,

> We must stop confusing religion and spirituality. Religion is a set of rules, regulations, and rituals created by humans which were supposed to help people spiritually. Due to human imperfection religion has become corrupt, politically divisive and a tool for power struggle. Spirituality is not theology or ideology. It is simply a way of life, pure and original. Spiritually is a network linking us to the most Higher power, the universe.

There are too many unstable countries with nuclear weapons. North Korea shoots missiles recklessly over neighboring Japan. Kim Jong-un, the leader of that rogue nation, wants to start World War III. Mankind will be decimated from the planet Earth through his ignorance and greed. An eye for an eye leaves one blind, and a tooth for a tooth eventually leaves one toothless. Every religion professes a true love for God yet religious fanatics will start wars to convince their masses of their correct philosophy. Why wars? Why not peace? Why not preach religious tolerance.

Peace does not come from the barrel of a gun. Peace comes through mutual respect, understanding, trust, love, sharing and cooperation for one another borders whether it is a neighbor or a country. There is only one God. He is called by many different names in several different religions. Strangely, "Thou shall not kill" is one of the most common commandments in every religious belief, yet people kill in the name of God. The Hindus call this present age, the Dark Age or the Age of Kali. The Dark Ages see the full ignorance of man and his barbaric atrocities to his fellow humans. The world will not end, but man will destroy humanity in a bid to prove their superiority or their stupidity. Mankind has become more educated with the advancement of science. However, education does not bring common sense or compassion. That education is been used to build stronger and more lethal force to destroy one another.

At present, there are more weapons of mass destruction to totally decimate life from Mother Earth. At present, we need wise, strong, and humble leaders with loads of common sense that is not forthcoming. As the world has become more educated and so-called civilized, we build more walls around our lives to keep neighbors and families at a distance. We are building emotional jails around ourselves and our immediate families. A quote from J. Krishnamurti says,

> When you call yourself an Indian or a Muslim or a Christian or anything else, you are being violent. Do you see why it is violent? Because you are separating yourself from the rest of mankind. When you separate yourself by belief, by nationality, by tradition, it breeds violence. So a man who is seeking to understand violence does not belong to any country, to any religion, to any political party or partial system; he is concerned with the total understanding of mankind.

When I was a young boy growing up in Trinidad, the people were kind, caring, and sincerely loving. They were honestly sincere in their desire to support friends and neighbors, yet the majority were materially poor. Everyone shared their measly food like they were family. There was no difference between Christians, Muslims, and Hindus. Religion and race did not divide neighbors. Everybody was one big, happy family. Fifty years later, what really happened to that joy and happiness? This despair is happening in every corner of the globe. People at present live in concrete jungles without knowing their neighbors. Families live like enemies. Thanksgiving Day and similar holidays are occasions to share and be happy, yet families celebrate alone. Countries throughout the world spend more money on military hardware and wars than buying much needed foods for their starving people. The rich get richer, and the poor become more impoverished. I guess the road to hell is paved with many good intentions.

This book is dedicated to the desperate journey of millions of immigrants throughout the world who sacrificed their lives in search of peace, harmony, and a better way of life. Sometimes in life, you think the grass is greener on your neighbor's side, but there are many hidden thorns.

Every so often, life is just an illusion meant to flatter or deceive you. Here are my humble suggestions to avoid mass migration to my world leaders:

1. Leaders must treat their citizens like they would treat your own family. Sorry, that statement is partly

incorrect because some families live like enemies. Leaders should treat their people with love and mutual respect.

2. Leaders must be held accountable for any unjustified aggressions of war. Many Americans believed that the Iraqi war was unjustified. Was it started to promote American interest in the Middle East? Hugo Chavez in Venezuela ruined his country, experimenting with socialism. A once prosperous nation has left its people begging for food and basic amenities. Haiti followed the same suicidal path as Venezuela. Dictators should be a word of the past.

3. The constitution of every country should not allow any leader to serve more than two terms in office.

4. Democracy should reign supreme to avoid religious fanatics or communist regime. Democracy is a government elected by the people for the people not through the barrel of a gun.

5. Elected leaders have a unique responsibility to be fathers and mothers of their nations. They must be held accountable for their mistakes and injustices.

6. The United Nations must play a more active role in the aggression of countries. A country's borders must be respected by neighboring countries. The United

Nations must impose crippling and mandatory punishment for invading countries. Freezing the assets and the bank accounts of teachers of its leaders hurts their wallets.

7. Parents, do not leave education totally in the hands of teachers. True education begins at home. It is a 24-7 permanent job. Teach your children to dream big. The skies are the limit to their every ambition. Every dream can become a reality. This may be a little comical. Some parents were appealing to their school board to ban their children from getting homework. They whine that homework is equivalent to child labor, and these assignments are too tough on their delicate minds and body. Parents, please play an active role in the lives of your children. Be their mentor; become their close friend and confidant. Guide them on life's desperate journey, and you will reap good rewards.

The story is told about a divorced father who, after work, was so tired that he never played games or spoke with his only child unless it was absolutely necessary. The court had ruled that his drunken mother was totally unfit, so he had no choice but to accept custody of this unfortunate child. As days passed by, they became strangers living under the same roof. One day at school, he was given an assignment to write about the sport baseball. He knew nothing about the sport. So he wrote the following statement to his teacher: "It was raining heavily. Therefore, baseball was not possible for a long time, maybe for the full season of it. I think the monsoon rains of India has come to Florida." We may laugh at this joke. It is funny.

Here is another one for your reading pleasure. Janice was a cute and smart child. One day, the teacher smiled and said, "Janice, dear, can you stand and tell the class what you will like to be besides a human? You can name a thing, animal, or your favorite pet like a dog."

Without any hesitation, the little girl jumped to her feet quickly. She blurted out, screaming, "A cell phone!"

The teacher was confused but pleasantly curious at her answer. She smiled at the little girl. "Pray tell, why a cell phone?"

The little girl innocently answered with a broad smile, "My parents are talking on their cell phone all the time. They are always on Facebook and Twitter with their friends. They never pay attention to me. When I interrupt them, they angrily tell me that they are on their phone. They usually get very upset. My mommy says that is impolite to disturb her when she is on her precious cell phone. I was thinking that maybe if I was a cell phone, I would get some attention." Everyone laughed, but it was indeed sad but true.

Finally, a teenage daughter asked her father how much he works for by the hour. Her father told her fifteen dollars per hour. She told him she wanted to borrow fifteen dollars. He inquired why she wanted the money. Her answer was genuinely simple: she wanted to pay him for one hour of his time to spend with her.

Everyone will find those stories very funny. Are they true in your life? Then why is your most precious investment in your life neglected? Are we leaving our children's future in the hands of their teachers and policemen?

The story is told about a father who never paid attention to his only son. When his son turned eighteen years old, he started drinking heavily with a gang of alcoholic friends. His father had a stroke and was disabled for life. One day, he begged his son, "My precious son, can you bring a glass of water, please. I am thirsty."

His drunken son looked at the father. "Not now, old man. I am busy. My friends are waiting for me. Get it yourself."

A child is not guilty for the few moments of passion or sins of the parents. Spend time with them and build them a strong foundation on life's journey. Make them a part of your life not a burdensome task. Become a part of their everyday lives. Nourish their roots with good parental nutrition. They will have deep roots with strong family values.

Parents, ensure that your children are educated to the tertiary level. Education is the cornerstone for success in their lives. Education is the salvation from poverty and darkness. Education liberates them from the shackles of slavery and the bonds of poverty. Love is giving your children "time-out" or discipline. Without the suitable discipline, there is no direction or purpose. The good book says, "Do not spare the rod and spoil the child."

There is a story that is told about a rich man's son who was just about to graduate from a prestigious college. Many months before graduation, his son nagged his father for a new and expensive car. After graduation, the father called his son into his office to congratulate him.

He was a proud father. His father presented him with an expensive leather-bound journal. The son was very angry with the ailing father. He became verbally abusive. He threw the journal and slammed the door as he left the room. He never spoke to or visited his father after that day. He focused on getting rich and raising his own family.

One day, he received a letter stating that his father had passed away. His stubborn father was cremated by his only servant. His father had left all his wealth to his only son. In his father's office, he came across the same journal that his father had attempted to give him at his graduation. As he flipped through the pages, a golden car key dropped from the back of the journal. A dealer tag read, "My loving son, wherever this car takes you, remember me. I love you, Son. I grew up in a family where there was no love. You are always in my heart. Do not be like me—loveless. I am dying, Son. Love always. My journey in life is completed, yet there is no love between us. I love you. Your dad." Whatever comes your way, be thankful. There are millions of people who cannot get one decent meal per day.

Parents, it is very important to teach your children to be humble yet strong. For example, be humble when you are given a ticket for a wrongful speeding violation. However, be strong to go to court and contest that ticket. There is an appropriate time and place to address all social injustice. Peaceful protests are productive within the confines of the law. Peaceful protests can bring meaningful changes. Remember Mohandas Gandhi non-violent protest against British rule led to a free and independent India. Protests are very healthy processes for a democratic society. Take a detour when life's roadblocks appear suddenly. Do not be afraid to build and travel on a new road in your life. Remember, to err is human. Everyone makes mistakes.

Become part of the solution in society not the problem. You can make a substantial difference in someone's life.

Religious teaching and prayers must be a necessity in all schools at all levels. We must learn about every religious ideas and cultures. Ignorance brings hate. Understanding one another's culture and values promote tolerance and understanding of one another's diverse culture. It will outshine ignorance and mistrust. It will promote goodwill among different ethnic backgrounds.

A good moral upbringing taught by the parents is another criterion for success. When you are angry as parents, do not make statements to your children such as "You are stupid and lazy like your father. He is a no-good man." Teach your children to be humble, respectful, but strong. They must be taught to obey the laws of the land. A tree with roots that is nourished with love bear much fruits of compassion and tolerance. Let them understand that parents are our first creator, and the road to heaven is at the humble feet of our parents.

We must have a good relationship with our neighbors again. They can play a key role in your child's development. Invite them to your home to share a meal. When you have any problems or good news, share it with them. Make your neighborhood safe again.

Let us be kind and loving human beings again. Material wealth that we crave so madly for is but an illusion or *maya*. We came into the world with nothing, and we leave with nothing. Share your love with a smile. Mother Teresa said, "It is not how much we give but how much love we put into giving. Let us make one point, that we meet one another with a smile, when it is difficult to smile."

This book seeks to unite people in their journey in life. Desperate journey is the struggle of mankind to adapt to the ever-changing environment. Life's journey is not only about your goals and destination but also about the precious moments that you create along the way. A quotation from Jenny Perry states, "I am in competition with no one. I run my own race. I have no desire to play the game of being better than anyone, in any way, shape or form. I just aim to improve, to be better that I was before. That's me."

Create your own path to success, and your life's journey will be complete. Remember, home is where the heart feels loved. Home is where there is peace, harmony, and tranquility. Home is where there is a shelter or safe harbor from the violent storms of life. Home is a country where there is freedom from oppression. Make an impact in your surroundings. Life is short and precious; make every moment count. Life is a challenge; complete it. Our world has changed but not for the betterment of society as Chris

Hedges lamented, "We now live in a nation where doctors destroy health, lawyers destroy justice, universities destroy knowledge, governments destroy freedom, the press destroys information, religion destroys morals, and our banks destroy the economy."

Changes in your life begin one step at a time. Desperate journey is a gamble to make life more comfortable. After all, the grass always looks greener on your neighbor's side. Our journey continues contemplating life. I was contemplating about life.

CHAPTER TWO

Our Journey Begins
With One Step

Naturally, I am a very positive person. I always wear that positive smile on my face. It is real, and even my underwear has a smiley face. Red is my favorite color. It is bright and zestful like my profession, which is providing answers and comfort to my depressed patients. In my life, my cup is always half full and not half empty despite grievous circumstances. You can best describe me as a jolly old fellow.

My name is Jonathan Cook. I am a practicing Psychiatrist by profession. Recent circumstances have drastically changed my outlook in life. My jolly temperament fears the thought of dying too soon. My life's ambitions are not yet accomplished. I am a contented man, and in terms of wealth, I am a rich man. My family owns a striving restaurant and a medical clinic. However, wealth without health is no good. I have a very devoted family but no grandchildren to spoil rotten.

When unexplained diseases start to cripple your body, your concept of life somewhat changes. My neurologist had first diagnosed me with the crippling multiple sclerosis. A few months later, he reevaluated and changed his diagnosis to amyotrophic lateral sclerosis or ALS, polymyositis, or maybe a combination of all. I sarcastically called him a practicing physician. He was still practicing getting his diagnosis correct. Was he guessing or practicing at my expenses? Sadly, he offered me no hope or had no sympathy for my diagnosis. I was just a number on his daily schedule. It was like listening to God issuing his last proclamation to mankind. He declared, "You have about two years to live more or less. Put your house in order. ALS is a killer. This disease is rapidly progressive that attacks the nerve cells responsible for controlling voluntary movement like your muscles. Enjoy life while you are healthy. Live like there is no tomorrow. I am sorry that it is deadly and crippling. Soon you may be confined to a wheelchair. Your speech may be affected or incoherent even to close family. Motor neuron diseases are difficult to diagnose, and there are not many options for treatment."

His face was turned away from me. With a half-smile, I blurted out sarcastically, "Doctor, what is the bad news that you have for me?" He looked at me, stone-faced and very confused. He did not get my weird sense of humor at a serious time. He was very brief and to the point as he hurriedly left from his office to visit another patient. There was no smile or comforting words from my doctor. His mood was somber and, I guess, very professional. I was flabbergasted to say the least at this time. As I left his office, I wanted to find a way to prove that my doctor's diagnosis was completely wrong. In the back of my mind, there was truth in his diagnosis. My legs were becoming extremely weak. My thigh muscles are now stiff, cramping, and painful. Walking is very challenging for me. My two legs have no coordination. My right leg is now literally very sluggish.

Diseases will change your perspective on life. The frail human body deteriorates very rapidly with incurable diseases. My friendly smile disappeared as I slowly departed from my doctor's office. My neurologist changed my prescription medications. He said that this new drug called rilutex promises great hope for my condition. It will cause my body cells to live longer by providing more oxygen to the nerves. That was very good. However, he warned me of some minor side effects. Constipation is a minor one compared to constant coughing, cancer, weight gain, nausea, vomiting, sleepless nights, chest pains, and horrid nightmares. It may cause death, a minor side effect. The minor side effects seem to outweigh the benefits of my medication. Rilutek was not a cure. As I drove to my workplace, I wondered why in heaven's name should yours truly be taking such a drug. Does my doctor know what is best for my medical condition? As practicing doctors, we are not gods, but sometimes we behave like we know it all. We are humans with a little more university education but more often no common sense or compassion. As I left my neurologist's office in Kendall, my legs started to behave listless and felt weaker and weaker. I contemplated whether to call for an assistance, Uber taxi service, or my wife, Anita. In the end, I decided to drive cautiously and slowly to my medical office. Driving my old SUV was proving recently to be quite a very challenging and dangerous task.

I was too lazy to upgrade my ride. On approaching Florida's Turnpike, I felt faint and lost consciousness for a few seconds. Was it a longer time? I woke up very drowsy. My head slumped against my steering wheel. I remembered taking one or maybe two Ambien tablets at bedtime. Then, I realized that my vehicle was neatly wedged in between two side railings. To make my situation worse, a policewoman was standing outside my vehicle. I placed my hands on my steering wheels as a precaution against any threat that the officer may perceived to her. I did not want to get shot accidentally for no apparent reason. She introduced herself very politely but with a sarcastic smile. "That was some nice driving, sir. You must be having a good day. My name is Officer Sandy. Are you okay? How much alcohol did you drink today?" She directed my eyes to her name tag that was neatly pinned on her left voluptuous large breast. As a man, it was impossible not to notice them.

After closely reviewing her name tag, I stuttered then blurted without thinking, "I noticed that my response time was somewhat diminished. Drivers in Miami have a tendency to change lanes without any warning. I clearly saw a female driver changed lanes abruptly then steered directly in front of me. Then without warning, she pressed on her brakes. By mere instinct, I steered my vehicle to the present position to avoid rear-ending her car. From my vehicle, I could clearly see a cell phone in the driver's hands. You know those people. Anyway, Officer Sandy, everyone uses cell phones while driving in Miami. I tried to avoid hitting her car and ended up here."

Officer Sandy smiled calmly. "Sir, I was in the back of your car. There were no cars behind you. What did you mean by those people? Do you have a prejudice against women drivers? Are you okay to drive? Can I see your driver's license?" On examining my driving permit, her facial expression changed when she realized that she was one of my patients more than two years ago. At that time, she was passing through a bitter divorce. She gently handed me my documents then added with a radiant and sexy smile, "Doctor, please be safe on the road. Have a good day. I just got an urgent call of a bank robbery in progress.

I must go. Be safe on the busy roadways." She hastily departed with her siren blaring loudly.

After an hour of near misses of accidents, sweltering heat, and traffic jam, I finally reached my office. My work in the field of psychiatry is recognized internationally. Since our last pleasant meeting, my family and our restaurant have grown tremendously. One of my adopted sons, Tom, is also involved in my medical practice.

Tom is a fellow Psychiatrist. He is gay, a fact that I accepted for his life. My motto has always been that everyone has a unique journey in life. Tom jokingly believes that he knows more about medicine than an old veteran like me. He says teasingly that I have an old and outdated school thinking. Since Tom is involved in my medical practice, I decided to focus my time and energy in helping patients deal with the stress of living and adapting to a new country. Miami is a melting pot for refugees from all over the world, especially Central and South America. Crime, difficult economic times and kidnappings are major factors that contribute to their citizens making desperate journeys to the Unites States. Critics of Miami have said that the city does not represent true American culture and values. Internationally, this refugee crisis is proving to be a major headache for developing countries. I sat, idly relaxing, reading, and researching about ancient mass migration.

This phenomenon is not new to our modern world. It is as old as early civilization.

One of the earliest mass exoduses was from Asia to North America. It dates back more than twenty thousand years ago. The migrants traversed by foot through icy, frigid Russia, the Bering Straits, and into Alaska. Then, they settled throughout the Americas and the Caribbean. Despite the extreme forbidding climates, they sacrificed everything to start a new life. This ordeal was truly a desperate and historic challenge into uncharted and uninhabitable lands. These heroes came with nothing yet constructed a vast empire far superior to the Europeans at that time.

The Mayans from Mexico had an organized system of government equivalent to our modern civilization. They made the 365-day calendar year. They were the first to make chocolates and tortillas. They were knowledgeable about herbal medicine like the ancient Ayurveda medicines of India. Despite the genocide of their people, Mayan and Aztec architectures still stand proudly today as a distinguished civilization of their legacy. Their cultures were built with blood, sweat, tears, and sacrifice. Some of their legacies and ruins have been restored and are popular tourism sites in Central America, leaving an indelible stamp on ancient world history.

In the Americas, hundreds of millions of people were decimated from their own land. This was mass genocide before the word was introduced into the English language. However, history records that the Vikings had traveled by sea and traded with these native North American Indians five hundred years before Columbus had rediscovered the so called New World. Most history books do not mention that the Vikings left the American Indians in peace rather than conquer and plunder their lands. They became important trading partners.

As I am writing this book, my eyes strayed to my television of heart breaking news as Russian MiG fighter jets were bombing civilian refugees' safe zones in Syria. This tragic news immediately caught my eyes. Two of my children, Krishna and Lisa, were presently working in the war zone in refugee camps in Syria. Krishna and Lisa cared more for the other people's problems than their personal safety. They are volunteer nurses working for a medical organization called Volunteers for Humanity like Doctors without Borders or the Red Cross. Volunteers for Humanity were working selflessly in collaboration with the United Nations. I am not against their humanitarian effort. In fact, I admire the courage and fortitude of my children to sacrifice their lives to help others. Their hearts are certainly bigger than mine and certainly in the right place. My thoughts were torn for their utmost dedication to humanity and the bodily dangers that await them. However, the nightmares of my two angels being kidnapped weighed heavily on my soul. Kidnapping, mutilations, and beheadings of aid workers, especially American citizens, were proving to be a profitable business for terrorists in the Middle East. At night, I get these horrid nightmares about my children being kidnapped by terrorist organizations, or was it the unwanted side effects of my Ambien tablets and ALS medications? I get these horrid dreams of my daughter Lisa being beheaded and the terrorists laughing mockingly. In fact, my nerves are shaken every time the telephone rings. My heart starts to palpitate beyond my understanding. It has been reported that terrorists hide among the helpless refugees waiting for opportunities to strike at unsuspecting targets. They even have forged American passports.

However, the United States government has a strict policy that they do not negotiate with terrorists. The United Nations sadly cannot provide enough adequate security for their many volunteers. My mind was filled with bloody negative thoughts as I sat quietly in the solitude of my spacious office, awaiting consultation with my next patient. Today I wish that I were a patient. I wanted advice and comfort, knowing that the lives of my children could end at any moment. A caring parent's heart is never prepared to hear the tragic news of their children.

Today was a special day in my life. Krishna and Lisa were returning from war-torn Syria after two years of service. I could breathe a sigh of relief. In the newspapers, I read about women suicide bombers killing hundreds of innocent refugees, mainly women and children. Terrorists have shot down a commercial airline with 275 passengers over Syria and Egypt. Everywhere, there seems to be tragic news. I still think of my adult children as my little babies. They are more precious than all my material possessions. They are the jewels in my crown of life. I get very emotional when I mention my children. My childish behavior radiates around them. As Psychiatrists, we tell our patients to have a positive outlook on life. Negative thoughts harbor negative energy that can damage your health. As I spoke on the telephone, I noticed that my speech was slurred like a drunkard.

My walk was unsure and uneven. I fell to the floor. This was the first of many falls from the effects of a motor neuron disease. My ability to run very fast has become a thing of the past. Jogging was my leisure exercise, especially along the scenic Miami beaches, seeing numerous sexy bikini clad females from all over the world. It was surely a beautiful sight for sore eyes. Despite the recommended physical therapy, changes in my diet, and rigorous exercise, my body lacked the energy and stamina to function normally. Strangely enough, after my neurologist's new diagnosis, I decided that was certainly my last visit to his office. It was my childish decision, but I wanted to blame someone for my present predicament. Even as doctors, we behave immaturely or unprofessionally. When a problem affects you personally, professionalism flies out the window. Today my heart was not really focused totally on my patients.

The concepts of my ALS, migration, death, and the afterlife were becoming an obsession in my frantic search for answers. I wanted to learn more about the journey into the afterlife. After all, I felt that one of my feet was in the grave already. Was there life after death? However, I was determined to fight my sickness with my last breath of life. My life was becoming fruitful and worth living. After all, I had sacrificed and laid a solid foundation to ensure the material success of my family. My four children were adults now. They were all hardworking professionals. Tom and John are my adopted children. Anita, my wife, was formerly married to their father, Thomas. After a bitter divorce from their father, Anita fell in love with yours truly. "Where did you meet her?" you may inquisitively ask. She was a patient of mine. Love came to my office. You can safely joke and conclude that I mixed business with pleasure. Was it unprofessional or unethical, you may ask. It worked for me.

We fell in love and got married in that exotic island called Tobago. From that blissful marriage, we had two children. Krishna and Lisa are my nomadic children. From childhood, I instill in them the desire to help others. They are both registered nurses. John, my other adopted son, graduated in business administration. He and my wife Anita, his mother, managed our family restaurant. She boasted jokingly and sometimes seriously that her Miami-based international restaurant is unique in every way. She huffs and puffs her chest and says, "We are the best in the world. We are open twenty-four hours every day with live entertainment. We serve an international menu daily. Can you beat that?" No one answered or dared to contradict her strong words. On numerous occasions, my wife had mentioned to me, "Hey, baby, why don't you give up your medical practice and work for me? I can easily pay you twice the salary that you are making presently." I laughed because she intentionally forgot that I initially financed our restaurant. Nevertheless, she thumps her chest and proudly boasts, "I am the real boss." It does not matter; her happiness is what is important to me. You know what they say, "A happy wife, a happy life." Can you imagine giving up my medical practice to work in a restaurant?

Was working for my wife demeaning or practical? No way. My wife can be nagging and domineering. Would it be many wasted years of studying? She was certainly right and precise in our financial assessment. My medical practice was very popular but not that profitable. We were paying our bills on time yet not showing any huge profit margins like our restaurant. Insurance companies were paying meagerly returns for our hard-earned medical claims. My medical firm was sued on many occasions for frivolous matters. Thankfully, not only did we have a large malpractice insurance, but I also dipped into my personal savings account.

My greatest loss was when my patients died. For example, two of my elderly patients had died from a massive overdose of my prescription of OxyContin. On another occasion, a depressed Slovenian mail-order bride committed suicide by closing her garage door and leaving her vehicle on while asleep in the back seat. She died from carbon monoxide poisoning. Nevertheless, my medical practice was my legacy and contribution to mankind not just for monetary satisfaction.

My children were obedient and very respectful. This was a precedent that I instilled in their hearts from early childhood. They were taught to be respectful to everyone and be helpful to everyone. They were taught to call everyone *sir*, *mister*, or *miss* rather than their name. What more could a man want in his life? I dreamed about my children having to settle down and having a family of their own near my home. After all, I was not getting any younger. I wanted grandchildren to hug, cuddle, and spoil rotten with affection. I wanted time to spoil them silly.

Incurable diseases deliver a sad reality that death lurks around the corner in the twinkle of an eye. Incurable diseases hit you without warning like a thief in the night. You truly believe that your life is perfect, but some imperfection seeps in to make your life despondent.

My wife Anita called it exhaustion. She would not believe my neurologist's diagnosis. She jokingly said, "My love, go and see the world. You work more than sixty hours per week without proper compensation. Baby, you need a stress reliever, maybe a month vacation in Las Vegas." My wife was right at least this time. Women are always right. I was trapped between four walls, tirelessly working more than sixty hours weekly, caring for my depressed patients, yet ignoring my own health. There was no lunch break. There is an old saying that a mechanic doesn't have a working car, a painter's house is not painted, and a good doctor takes care of his patients more than themselves.

Tom entered my office without knocking. He said quietly, "Papa, why is your old SUV damaged? Anyway, you do have an appointment with a Cuban immigrant. I heard about the horrific bombings in Syria. Do not worry about Krishna and Lisa. There is nothing better in life than serving humanity. Their home is not only by your side but wherever God leads them. Suffering has no borders. It is compassion at its highest when their hearts drive your children on desperate journeys throughout the world. Papa, I remember what you tell your patients. Do not build bars around yourself. Eventually, you will put yourself in a jail in solitary confinement. Open the bars of your life and share that goodness with others. Enjoy yourself. Life is short. Therefore, enjoy life's journeys, and make every minute a memorable one. I know that you are too preoccupied with resolving every patient's illness. Who is looking after your health? No one."

Tears came to my eyes. He had analyzed my problem so professionally like his old mentor. I was very proud to call him my son. Tom has always been my comforter and my strength. I replied with a cunning smile. "Ah, my son. I forgot to tell you that Krishna and Lisa will be back in Miami from Syria. We will meet at our restaurant tonight. That is my good news."

CHAPTER THREE

The Cuban Migration: Is the Grass Greener on the Other Side?

I wanted to spend my afternoon session understanding the massive Cuban refugees' crisis in Miami through the eyes of one of their people. My patient had fled from the jaws of hell to seek political asylum in the United States. Since that time, he has been experiencing an emotional turmoil, trying to transition to the American way of life. To add fuel to the fire, his American wife had filed for divorce. To Jose, coming to the USA was like finding the golden city of El Dorado and that all his troubles were behind in communist Cuba. He cannot adapt to life in Florida even though he lives in a predominantly Hispanic area called Little Havana. I summoned Maria, my ever-smiling bilingual medical assistant, as my translator.

"*Hola*, Maria. Jose is my next patient. He will be bringing his six-year-old son with him. I may need your help with some Spanish translation. Please arrange for a babysitter for at least two hours in our conference room. I want to give him sufficient time to find concrete solutions to his problems.

"Dr. Tom, my son, I will see you later. Please, this is my final appointment for the evening. Remember, your brother and sister return from Syria tonight at Miami International Airport. I am literally dying to see them. It has been two years since I embraced them."

Tom hugged me very tightly. He looked into my eyes. "They are not only your treasures, but they are an important part of my life. I love them." He smiled broadly as he closed the door behind him.

My fingers cramped as I reached to access our computer health-care information about my new patient. Jose was born in Santiago de Cuba. It is the island's second largest city. It is a hot, hilly, and culturally diverse city. It explodes with many festivals, street vendors, horse-drawn carts, the sounds of salsa music, and the sights of white-garbed Santeria devotees. He came from a large family of thirteen siblings. He has ten brothers. They lived in a single-family government home with three small bedrooms located near a military base. Later that evening, Jose would jokingly tell me that his father had problems sleeping because of the constant noises coming from old Russian warplanes. There was no television set in our home. Couples spent more time in bed, hence a large family. Oral contraceptives were not readily available to everyone. All his brothers were affectionately named Jose, and his sisters were named Maria. I wondered what was the reason why. Was it a typographical error?

A few minutes later, my medical assistant Maria of Cuban descent reassured me that this was a cultural tradition. She said, "We like to keep a single name in our family. It is easy to remember. It is a tradition." I wondered whether she was serious or joking.

She escorted Jose Garcia with his son Jose into my office. From his body language, I could tell that he was forced into my office. He hesitantly walked like a loaded gun was pointed at his back. He was summoned in my presence for parenting, counseling, and mental evaluation by the children's foundation for abused children by the district judge. His wife Maria had petitioned the court that Jose was an irresponsible and a verbally abusive parent. Her husband was prone to the bouts of violent behavior and a bad-tempered father. He had displayed periodic violent tantrums even in the presence of their little child. In her court document, she filed a petition: "Sometimes you could not tell the difference in behavior between father and child. Both displayed childlike tantrums with violent episodes. I feel threatened and unsafe in the presence of my alcoholic husband. I am truly afraid for my life."

With these alleged threats, the court had issued a temporary restraining order against my patient. The judges, in their wisdom, tend to believe a woman in the sole interest of the welfare and safety of her child. Why does the court lean heavily against the father? There are many documented cases of physically abusive mothers. In divorce cases, the child or their pet animals are used as pawns to benefit both hostile parents. Love dies after divorce, resentment, pent-up rage, and hatred steps in its place. The innocent child suffers in silence, while their parents fight over the spoils of war or material gains. Nonetheless, Jose gently extended his callous hand. His handshake was strong like a handyman.

Maria, my assistant, sat on this session for much needed translation. He started to speak slowly, "Doctor, my English is not too good, but I will try." I smiled to reassure him that his language was not a problem. "This is a very informal and a relaxed consultation. Do not worry, my friend. You will do just fine. Jose, please be yourself, and tell me about your family. Do not worry. Most people in America do not speak proper English. You can speak about things which bother you. Your conversation will not leave this room. Everything that you say will be strictly confidential."

I stopped talking then smiled with reassurance. I reached unnoticeably for my notepad. Jose hesitated and gazed at the door. For a moment, I thought that he wanted to make a hasty dash and leave the room. He was unusually nervous and very disconcerted. His hands were sweating profusely. Nevertheless, he started to speak, "Hola."

I answered, "Hola," which means "hello" in Spanish. When you live in Miami, it is important that you must learn some Spanish. After all, some Americans jokingly refer to Miami as little Cuba. Maria smiled and continued to translate.

Jose continued, "My name is Jose. This handsome boy and the love of my life is my son, little Jose." He beamed with a utopic pride as he looked at his adorable son. Jose took a deep breath. "Coming to America was a nightmarish journey in desperation to escape from an unpopular and oppressed communist regime under the iron fist of Dictator Fidel Castro. However, living here in Miami has turned into a bigger nightmare. You see, Cubans live in a country that time and progress forgot for many years. Cuba is frozen in time. Here in America, people live in a modern world. Cubans live fifty-nine years backwards. For me, adaptation is very difficult with no family and friends to support you here in Miami. I made a desperate journey for freedom. Am I free? What is really freedom? Independence from oppression or living without love and not integrating into this great American dream? Despite the generosity from the United States government, my life in Miami has not been easy.

My six-year-old child does not speak proper English. In school, they talk to him in Spanish. At home, it is the same situation. I do not speak proper English so many people laugh at my accent. When I go to many places here, my first words are 'Habla español?' or 'Do you speak Spanish?' In Cuba, my profession was a mechanical engineer. However, when it was harvesting time for agricultural crops like sugarcane, every Cuban was required to help with reaping the crops. We had no choice in this matter. *Volunteer* is not a suitable word. It was mandatory. The Cuban economy depended heavily on the production of sugar. Here in America, you must be certified in every organization that you are working. You must be educated in every area here. America is so different. You must have a well-paying job to survive here. In Florida, I am nothing. I am like a grain of sand in a vast desert. I am lost. In Cuba, you are given handouts by the government even though it is a measly ration. We are even given meats by monthly ration. It is a small portion. However, you learned to survive with that measly chicken feed ration—"

I interrupted him. I wanted to learn more about his family. His conversation was getting to be more political. "Jose, my friend, please tell me about your family life in Cuba."

He paused for a moment to scramble his thoughts in some logical pattern. He looked thoughtfully at the door. He moved in the direction of the door. Maria eyed him closely. He turned around. "I am a political refugee living in Miami. I made that perilous journey many years ago in a makeshift raft from Cuba to Key West in Florida. Under the United States immigration laws called wet foot, dry foot policy for political refugees, Cubans can live in the United States as an American citizen. They must touch dry land in USA by any means at their disposal. Every Cuban knows this sacred law.

I lived in Cuba with my lovely wife and two teenage daughters. Compared with Miami, we lived in primitive conditions in a country that did not progress with time. Progress and modernization had left Cuba in the dark ages. Communist Cuban human rights violations were one of the highest in the world. Toilet paper is a luxury item in Cuba. Everything that we accept or take for granted in USA—like toothpaste, medicine, toiletries, and cornflakes— are very scarce in the island. When a hurricane hits the communist island, there is literally no food and drinking water for many days for the affected areas. This happens every year, sometimes more than three times in one year. It is a horrid nightmare. Life is difficult under an oppressive communist government. In Cuba, we like matching names.

My name is Jose. I fell in love with Josefina. There, I was married to a beautiful, sexy, voluptuous woman named Josefina. We were madly in love. We went everywhere together even to harvesting of the sugarcanes. Josefina and I became the best of friends. We were pals, buddies, and lovers. We were inseparable. We were truly in love. Partying by the beaches was a big event. There are not much social activities in Cuba, except for dancing and partying. We would invite our neighbors. We were all family. A family is expected to take care of one another. At the beach, we all got drunk from homemade alcohol. One day, in a drunken state, I dare or was boasting with some friends to sail to the freedom land. USA was called the land of milk and honey—the land that every Cuban is visualizing to migrate to improve themselves. We all jumped into the sea on my homemade raft without any thoughts of the dire consequences. We were six close friends. We loved each other like brothers. This episode started as a prank. Would it be our worst terrifying ordeal? The strong currents compounded with the high winds speedily carried our raft into the deeper waters further and further away from the land. My cousin Jose started to cry like a newborn baby. He shouted, 'Dos mio, mi amor Maria, donde esta, mi amor? Por favor, ven y salvarme' or 'My God, my love, Maria, where are you, my love? Please come and save me.'

The shoreline was slowly disappearing as we saw our frantic loved ones waving in the distance. Jose, my neighbor, screamed loudly. Was it a death scream? In desperation, he jumped into the rough, tempestuous waters, eager to swim ashore. In his quickness, he made one fatal error—he could not swim. Like a heavy rock and in the twinkle of an eye, he disappeared near our raft. He never reemerged. Everyone started to scream in disbelief. Our crew got sober quickly as our beloved Cuban shoreline disappeared in the horizon.

Our treasured Cuba was no more, never to return. If by a lucky coincidence we were to return to Cuba, then certainly, we will be guilty of deserting the communist regime. We would be labeled as deserters. All my families and friends will be simply thrown immediately in jail for life or even face a firing squad without a trial. It was a no-win situation from every angle. The surging currents quickly carried us into dangerous uncharted pathway. As the day dragged slowly by, we were greeted by some unwelcomed guests. The curious great white sharks were circling our ride. Their massive bodies miniaturized our raft. We pretended to play dead and keep our feet away from their reach. They were not an immediate threat, but the scorching heat was turning our raft to a fiery furnace. The great white sharks disappeared as they had appeared without any fanfare. Were they stalking us?

Our throats were sorely parched. We resorted to sign language for all communications. One day exposure to the scorching tropical sun, our bodies lied motionless. Our feet dangled in the cool water to calm our heated bodies. Day one was a painful nightmare as my one of my dear friends died from dehydration. We wept tearlessly as we pushed his stiff lifeless body into the choppy waters. We stared in horror as the ever-vigilant sharks made a cheerful feast of his mortal remains. Nighttime slowly crept on us. In the darkness of the moonless night, we were awakened by a loud ear-piercing scream like a thief in the night, a death cry that I felt unfathomable within my tired dying soul. My close friend and neighbor's feet were amputated with surgical precision by the sharp razor teeth of the great white predatory sharks. The dark, choppy water around our raft turned blood red. A great white shark had extricated both legs in the twinkle of an eye.

To this day, I wake up sweating profusely from this nightmare, a nightmare that was my fault alone. We heard some loud, sharp, and piercing cries for a few minutes, then an unnerving deadly silence. That night, we prayed to any and every saint known to the Roman Catholic faith. The extravagant wraths of Mother Nature were alive and were been dished out to us. We experienced extremes of temperatures from the sweltering sun during the daylight hours to frigid icy winds at night. Day two, the sun had risen in all it's blazing glory. It was a euphoric sight. The sea was calm with a soothing westerly breeze. At the break of dawn, we were greeted by the sight of those magnificent mammals of the sea, the so-called killer whales. There were three of them. Was it a family unit? Mom, Dad, and their calf. They kept nudging our raft in a northwesterly direction. The gigantic whales were in a playful and lively mood. Their tearful, watery eyes indicated to us that they could not help our plight. Later in the cool and breezy morning, a band of playful dolphins joined in the fun, jumping near our raft. They were our company for the morning of day two. Were they guarding us against the great white sharks' vicious attacks? My sea friends waved their enormous tails as they bade farewell.

In the evening of day two, I joked with my two accomplices to preserve our sanity. We made silly promises like alcohol and seawater will not be mixed ever again to all my Roman Catholic saints. As the sun was rapidly sinking in the horizon, a speedboat docked alongside our battered raft. The three of us pretended to be lifeless. The pirates boarded our raft and caressed our frail bodies with their sharp, long machetes. They removed all our jewelry one by one. Juan, my brother, grimaced in pain, was shot instantly. His body was tossed into the sea. Fidel and I remained still and silent. Was this really happening? Was I dreaming? Was it a mirage? Was it a fantasy of my intense imagination? In Cuba, as children, we had been told of numerous stories of modern-day pirates roaming the high seas. They seized every fisherman boat engines. The pirates speedily departed with all our worldly possessions with a deafening sound from their speedboat.

On our second night at sea, we saw several massive cruise ships cruising about a mile away from our raft. Their sounds of merriment revived our dying souls. We tried to remain inconspicuous from them. If they had spotted us, we would be immediately deported to Cuba. When we were thirsty, we drank our urine and perspiration for water. After three days at sea, our feeble bodies were looking like living corpses. I wondered whether this desperate journey was worth the high costs. Fidel and I were the only survivors of this horrifying ordeal. By some divine intervention, we were washed ashore in scenic Key West in Florida. We were treated as heroes by the Hispanic community of Miami for a few weeks. The media was kind to us for a few moments. I lied about my family to the immigration authorities. I renounced my family. I wanted to start a new life in Florida with no strings attached. After one year of pampering by the immigration authorities, they gave me my legal documents to live in USA permanently.

One month later, by the law of chance, a beautiful, ravishing, and voluptuous Maria bumped into me at the Dolphin Mall. I guess I am a lucky guy with the name *Maria*. Her beautiful innocence and her sexy smile is reminiscing of my amorous Cuban wife. My male hormones were strong for the company of a beautiful, sexy woman. Her family were originally from Venezuela and Dominican Republic. Sometime later, I learned that she was an illegal alien hiding from the immigration authorities called ICE. Her tourist visa had expired. Maria was very street smart. Miami is considered a sanctuary city. A sanctuary city adopts local policies designed not to prosecute immigrants solely for being illegally in the USA. President Trump sort to reverse those policies. Maria intermingled perfectly with her Hispanic culture and community in Miami. Everyone protected their people from the authorities. Maria, strangely enough, fell head over heels in love with me in the blink of an eye from the moment our paths crossed. Was it a deception or true love? I was truly flattered. I believed that I had won the lottery when I encountered Maria. After all, I am not handsome man like Brad Pitt but a potbelly, chubby short man with some receding hairline. My attire was not impressive. They were secondhand clothing bought at the Goodwill store near my home. I theoretically assumed that our similar Hispanic culture must be the reason to have a successful relationship. Was I mistaken in my narrow-minded thinking? There were so much diverse, sexy, different ethnic single women in Miami. Why did I choose this Hispanic woman? It was my simple reasoning We ate rice, black beans, yucca, and pork. After all, the way to a man's heart was through his stomach. Every day, we enjoyed the same type of foods at different Hispanic restaurants. My new love affectionately called me babe. I felt loved, wanted, and special. My heart skipped a beat when that loving word resonated from her sexy lips.

"Maria was admired by everyone for her dancing skills. Her aficionados said her waist gyrated in circles like they were made of rubber. Her dance moves were erotic and provocative. Dances like merengue, bachata, salsa, and tango were not foreign to her. Maria was the darling of the dance floor. Her sexy and sensual moves dominated every nightclub. Strangely enough male patrons everywhere knew Maria by name. Was I just too dumb, love-stricken or too pigheaded to comprehend that I was been used a tool of convenience? The heart can mislead a man of the truth. One day like a bolt of lightning, my love hit me with these frightening words—'Mi amor (or *my love*), I am pregnant with your baby. We must get married at once. My parents must not know about this pregnancy. They truly believe that I am still a virgin.' Like a dumb, novice schoolboy, I was lost for words. I stammered, 'But... but... my love. How did it happen? We made love one time only, and you were menstruating. We use a condom also.' Maria gently caressed my nipples. She looked into my eyes very tenderly. 'No man has ever been inside of me except you. This is your baby. This is our baby. I love you.' Her words were heartwarming, genuine, and convincing with tears in her innocent eyes. One week later, after her shocking announcement, we were married in the courthouse in downtown Miami. Fidel was my best man. It was a somber celebration like a funeral. My new bride insisted that there was no time to go on a honeymoon. She jokingly added, 'You want to kill my baby. Abstinence from sexual intercourse is good during pregnancy.' Apart from being a party animal, my love was an astute scholar. She was studying for her medical board examination. Now it was customary in the company of her male friends. My wife spoke English only. Stupid me, I smiled or nodded like I understood their conversations. When they laughed, I laughed louder.

As a Cuban political refugee, I was given a house at a very reduced price by the US government. Shortly afterwards, my wife became an American citizen by our marriage. I was ecstatic and overpowered with joy. Finally, everything appeared perfect in my life or a calm before a storm."

Jose stopped his conversation to inquire about the welfare of his son. My assistant showed him the television monitor with both my coworker and his son snoring and fast asleep. Jose finally smiled as he looked closely at the television screen. He slowly sipped some Cuban coffee and continued, "My mother in Cuba had said that in the beginning of a marriage that a new broom will sweep clean. Anyway, we spent every weekend partying at our home at my expense. Maria's family loved to roast a whole pig. However, after Maria became an American citizen, her family became openly hostile near me. I was unemployed. They called me in Spanish *perezoso* or 'lazy.' I ask myself, Why should I work when the United States government was giving me free food, housing, and money every month by virtue of being a political refugee from Cuba? Nevertheless, Maria studied all day and night. Her ambition superseded her pregnancy to qualify as a medical doctor. She became less affectionate towards me or just ignored me. Shortly afterwards, Maria qualified as a medical intern. By virtue my unemployment status, I was converted to a full-time housekeeper and her housemaid. I cooked, washed, and cleaned every day so there were no distractions for my adorable wife. I proudly said to myself, 'One day soon, there will be a doctor in my house.

My sacrifice will be worth it.' I was a gratified to be a doctor's husband and, but most important, a proud father to be called *papi* in my new country. One rainy evening, baby Jose came into the world without fanfare or joy from Maria's family. Nevertheless, he was my bundle of joy. Maria became depressed, withdrawn, and dejected. She displayed her fiery temper daily. Was my loving wife overworked and stressed from her hectic medical program and pregnancy? During her frequent episodes of violent tantrums, she broke everything in sight. I kept my distance and suffered in silence. When she said jump, I replied, 'How high, my love?'

After her pregnancy, my wife's fresh look in bed was proudly sporting her big tight granny panties and matching bras at bedtime. Our intimate moments were confined to a peck on my cheeks. I got the subtle and silent message that married men have learned to read between the lines since the beginning of time. You can watch but not touch. Wives use their emotions and lovemaking like a two-edged sword. However, in contrast, she wore her sexy Victoria's Secret underwear to her workplace. Nevertheless, there was calming solace in the room next to baby Jose that offered me a few moments of tranquility and serenity. In those moments of deep reflection in Cuba, my wife was so peaceful, loving, caring, and comforting. Her smile was contagious. I miss her dearly. Karma is a bitch or, as the saying goes, 'What goes around comes around.' In Miami, one day in deep distress, I spoke to my wife's Dominican sister about my wife's change in her personality. She literally bit my head off instead of words of consolation. She scolded me like one of her many children in the presence of her father. She growled, 'You are not a member of our family. You are not one our people. Maria's family is her brothers and sisters first and foremost in her life. In our eyes, she can do no wrong. You are not my children's grandfather. In fact, I demanded that my children call you Señor Jose, not Abeulo or Grandfather. A strong man can surely handle a robust woman. You are a weak, worthless, and an unemployed refugee. Our family fights like cats and dogs. We bitch and fight like animals, but in the end, family is family. No family is perfect.' "I was traumatized by her verbal abuse. How could I answer her cruel statements? For a few nail-biting moments, I was speechless. I briskly walked away without saying a word towards my flower garden. Her father, Juan, followed closely behind me. In my multicolored garden, tears flowed from my eyes. Juan placed his frail hands on my shoulders. He said apologetically, 'My son, I am sorry. When my children were young, they were very loving. Now there is no control over their nasty behavior. Women are very liberated in America. You must learn to live with these frequent outbursts. I have turned a deaf ear to it a lot of times. Every time I give advice, they laugh at me. They say that I am old school. I am sorry, Son. You have a good soul. One day Maria will regret her nasty behavior before it is too late.'

"Juan, unfortunately, was an avid smoker. A few weeks later, after our first and last encounter, Juan died from a massive heart attack. Maria was quiet about his passing. Thereafter, our conversations as husband and wife were fewer and fewer. I was afraid to speak to my wife. All my words sounded like an argument to her ears. My darling wife spent many hours talking and laughing on her cellphone in English. I was a willing prisoner entombed in my home with a suspected cheating and depressed wife with her baby. Could Jose be another man's child? That allegation frightened me.

"As baby Jose became older, his personality did not resemble any of our Hispanic origin. I thought that was very interesting. With each passing day, little Jose sounded like a truly white American. Could I discuss my doubts with my wife? Negative ideas confused my mind. Was our marriage a charade, a marriage of convenience, a necessary but evil strategic play for the sole motive for my wife to attain her American citizenship? Whenever, I opened my mouth, my wife would say that I was a worthless son of a bitch. Everything that came out of my lips was considered a heated argument to my darling wife. However, she spoke frequently and joyfully on the telephone for hours like she had verbal diarrhea to her family and many friends. Our baby became my sole responsibility. As Maria fired her scorching temper on me, screaming on the top of her voice, 'If you had kept your pants on, I will never be pregnant. You are the damn cause for my depression and mood swings. You put this baby in me in my moment of indiscriminate passion. Therefore, the damn baby is your sole responsibility. It is your baby. Take care of the damn thing.'

"Maria was acting like a raging bull. I remained silent at her coldhearted and insensitive remarks. She was deadly serious and intimidating. My brain froze for a few minutes as I resorted to digest her heart-wrenching words. One day, the revolting smell of fried fish filled our home. Baby Jose started to cry because of the stifling smoke emanating from my cooking. He started to cough incessantly. I thought it was a clever idea to open the front door to allow the fresh air to come inside my home. Baby Jose crying did not stop. I hurriedly took my baby outside of our little house. Strangely, in my poor neighborhood in Little Havana, there was a new posh car parked outside my home. It was a new Lamborghini from what I had read in sports magazines. The sweet and erotic sounds of sweet samba music were booming from inside the car. The glass was very dark tinted. Out of curiosity, I walked up slowly and stealthily towards the car. There were numerous burglaries in this neighborhood in recent times. Maybe it was a stolen vehicle. I was shockingly surprised to see my loving wife locked in a mouth-to-mouth passionate kiss with a white American man. I knocked angrily on the car door. The driver managed a sheepish smile and shamefacedly said 'hola' or hello with a strong American accent. He was a white American, a 'gringo,' as we Cubans would describe him. Maria was totally embarrassed. From my vantage point, her red sexy Victoria's Secret underwear was clearly visible. There was no secret here. Her face was red with anger. His hand was caught in the cookie jar. My wife hastily departed from the car. Blood rushed to my brain as I shouted angrily, 'Why the hell were you kissing that gringo? You had your tongue straight down in his throat!'

Maria became very aggressive. She turned to face me. Without any warning, her right hand ripped into my face. I held on tightly to baby Jose to avoid him falling to the ground. She followed with a kick to my groin. I saw stars in the daytime from that low blow. My face hit the ground solidly as my mouth kissed the concrete sidewalk. My front teeth were broken with the sudden and violent impact. Blood gushed from my mouth. The car sped away. Maria firmly placed her left shoe on my head and yelled at the top of her voice, 'Mi amor, my love, that is how we greet people in our culture. My love, I always tell you time and time again, you can leave me anytime with your son. That rich and handsome guy that you saw is my partner in the hospital. He gives me a ride every day to and from my work. He is a medical doctor. Remember, we have no vehicle. He can give me a ride anytime. Someone in this home must work so that we can survive. I am truly ashamed to have you as a husband. You are an embarrassment to me and my family.'

"Her loud, brash, and vicious antics had aroused the curiosity of our neighbors. They were standing in front of my house. They were prying but keeping their distance. Maria mockingly raised her middle finger at them in defiance. She shrugged and shook her head arrogantly as she hastily headed inside our home—"

I abruptly interrupted Jose as I rushed to the bathroom. Jose paused for a minute. His voice trembled with fear. As a practicing psychiatrist, this was truly a heartbreaking account of a neglected and abused husband. He shouldered his suffering in silence like an honorable man. A few minutes later, I motioned my patient to continue his story. Jose continued, "For five consecutive weeks, Maria did not speak to me. She was punishing me with her silent treatment. However, she ravenously ate all my tasty Hispanic meals. My loving wife showed no remorse for her unladylike behavior. When her family or friends came for a visit, she was the most loving wife and mother. She was an angel like a Mother Teresa. When they departed, the devil had possessed her. Were her mood swings a sign of a deep disturbed bipolar behavior like the classic Dr. Jekyll and Mr. Hyde? One day, my loving wife wrote a formal statement to me. 'Dear Mr. Jose, I am going to spend this weekend with my family in West Palm Beach. You are not invited. Therefore, you will have to take care of baby Jose.' Strangely, her family lived in poor little Havana but not in posh West Palm Beach. Those weekends, she bluntly stated, were her family time without her husband and child. During her so-called family weekends, she never answered her cell phone. I had no friends in Miami except Fidel, but he lived in Hialeah. Nevertheless, I retreated to the comfort of my kitchen to attend to my cooking, a Cuban cigar, and plenty of alcohol. On the weekend that Maria was allegedly visiting her family, I went to Homestead to gamble in cock fighting, accompanied by baby Jose and Fidel. This sport made me reminisce of my beloved Cuba. I started drinking alcohol more than my daily intake of water. In my drunken state while roasting a whole pig, I severely burned my right hand. Then it dawned upon me that consuming alcohol was not the solution to my problem. In fact, Maria ensured that my home always had a good stock of alcohol more than food. In my many drunken state, my loving wife would calmly say to me, 'Why the hell don't you kill yourself or drown in any one of the many lakes in Miami?'

At home, she never acknowledged the many cries of her son, 'Mama, Mama, Mama' with his tiny outstretched hands and innocent heavenly screams for a hug. I begged lovingly, 'Baby, the door is locked. Please open it. We must stop this constant fighting. I love you. Your baby is crying for you.' There was complete silence. I waited patiently for an answer that would not come from my hot-tempered wife. Then I heard that familiar loud snoring but irritating sounds coming from inside her room. I realized that my stressed wife had fallen into a deep slumber. I retired to the adjacent room to attend to little Jose. He fell asleep on top of my bulging belly."

Jose spoke about his ever-recurring nightmares of his desperate and perilous excursion to Florida from his homeland. He vividly remembered Fidel who was his comedian. "He jokingly asked, 'Why is it that Cuba never won a gold medal in swimming at the Olympics?' No one knew the answer, or maybe we were too weak to answer. Then he blurted out a comical answer, 'It is because all the good swimmers have already swum to America.' Our throats were parched, but we laughed. Our desperate journey for freedom had been achieved at an excessive cost. Four of my dear friends perished into the treacherous waters. Fidel and I were the only survivors. We became brothers for life, and he was my only faithful friend in America. Unfortunately, one year later, he was killed in a senseless drive by shooting in Hialeah."

I interrupted Jose that his son had awoken and was crying. Their interaction was valuable in my assessment of the case. As his son entered my office, he rushed to warmly embrace his troubled father. Their bond was real, emotional and unbreakable. Everyone was moved to shed tears. As little Jose spoke, his voice and accent were not typical of Hispanic descent. His father was correct in his assessment of his child. After a short break, little Jose departed with my assistant. I told the father to continue his story. He gladly obliged after seeing his son.

"One day, two police officers came to my home. They dragged me to spend the weekend in jail for alleged child abuse. I was fingerprinted and beaten like a common criminal. I spent three nights among seasoned criminals. At my divorce hearing, I represented myself. Money was scarce after all my savings went toward Maria's education and her parties at my home. Maria entered the courtroom while being consoled by her American Lamborghini driver. She had appointed a high-profile divorce lawyer that made mincemeat of my unprofessional arguments and my unemployment status. Her lawyer painted a gloomy and shady picture of me as a no-good unemployed drunken bastard, a child abuser, and an addicted gambler. Despite having no previous criminal record, he said firmly that I had been physically and mentally abusive to my devoted wife. At the hearing, the American judge directed one question toward, 'Do you speak English?' Thereafter, he totally ignored my remarks. In the aftermath of my divorce, I lost everything. My house was given to my now ex-wife. However, I was given total custody of my little boy. Maria rejected custody of her only child. My dreams were shattered into every meaningless direction. My mind contemplated suicide, but then my precious son would have no one to love him. My desperate journey from Cuba had turned into a terrifying nightmare, but my fortitude to flourish was stronger than losing all my material possessions. I jokingly said aloud to myself, 'We Cubans can survive anywhere. After all, we survived the Castro regime with nothing.'

"This Cuban refugee was unemployed, penniless, and homeless with a six-year-old child. The court, in their infinite wisdom, did not take into consideration the living arrangements of my child. For the next few months, Fidel's old American car was my home. It was like a big, spacious room. We slept under the shining stars or the rain-filled nights. My days of living in Cuba were here again. To gain additional income, I sold bottled water near Kendall

Medical Hospital and Bird Road. After one year of sacrifice, I was able to rent a modest one-bedroom apartment in Hialeah. Little Jose was placed in a daycare. Adaptation takes time, patience, and sacrifice. The road to success is steep and difficult to climb, but anyone can prosper in America. My business expanded after six months. I employed another Cuban refugee named Manny. He was gay and joked that women were more complicated than men. We became a well-organized team. Manny paid half of my rent. We sold bottled water every day. He also acted as my babysitter. We were business partners, roommates, and best buddies. In our leisure time, we drank beer, roast pork, and reminisced about good old Cuba. We were happy and contented.

Time flew quickly. Little Jose was now eight years old. He excelled in school with exceptional grades. He spoke proper English with his Hispanic- American accent. My life was perfect, or was it the calm before the storm? Like a thorn in my butt, my ex-wife came back like a leech to suck the last pittance of dignity from my caring soul. Her loveless mandate was simple and direct. 'I demand total custody of my only son. It is not possible for me to have any more children. I am willing to give you one hundred thousand dollars cash, no questions asked. Just sign a legal consent form authorizing the custody transaction. If you fail to sign the legal documents, then I will fight in court like an angry pack of wolves. Believe me, you will lose everything in court. My shrewd lawyers will chew you to pieces.' My answer was simple and straightforward that my baby was not for sale. Maria and her boyfriend had built a lucrative medical practice with offices in Miami, West Palm Beach, and Fort Lauderdale. My meager savings would go toward my bloodsucking lawyers or liars. The sacrifice for my son was worth everything. One day before my appointed court date, someone threw garbage on my front lawn and sidewalk. Overnight, someone had slashed all my car tires and spray-painted obscene words on the doors. Uber taxi service came to my rescue. At the court hearing, my son and I were immaculately dressed in similar outfits. Maria arrived in the courtroom with her boyfriend. Her eyes were blood red. Her lawyers painted a bleak picture of my life. They showed photos of my unsanitary living environment. Her doctors testified that their client was depressed every day because of her son. His absence from her life was causing severe financial, emotional, and psychological loss to their client. The judge bought her lawyers' arguments hook, line, and sinker. However, I was given unlimited visitation rights at the convenience of Dr. Maria.

After years of peace, my life was completely derailed by a con artist. Every night, I cried like a baby. Maria was an ungrateful son of a bitch. One day, my only loyal refugee friend, Manny, mentioned something confidently in a whisper under the influence of alcohol. He said, 'My friend, accidents can happen in the blink of an eye. We can arrange an accident for your bitch just like in Cuba.' I laughed, but Manny was deadly serious. He waved his hand angrily to reinforce his bold plans. With tears in my eyes, I hugged my only devoted friend. Our bloodshot eyes met. I answered firmly, 'Regardless of the endless pressures that Maria has caused in my life, no harm must come to her. I did not create her life, so I cannot destroy it. Moreover, she was still the mother of my child.'

In any event, my money-hungry lawyer had requested a paternity test to determine whether I was the father of our child. Here are the results. I cannot understand the medical language. 'Por favor traduce,' or please translate to make me understand." He smiled confidently as he gently placed the documents in my hands. Tension filled the room. For a few minutes, I shrewdly poured over the legal documents. After listening to Jose's story, I was not surprised at the findings. The documents stated explicitly that Jose, my client, was not the biological father of Maria's child. A different and clearer picture was now immerging. Maria had used Jose as a tool to finance her studies and take care for her child. In addition, she became an American citizen by her marriage to Jose. I looked at Jose with sorrow and sadness in my heart. Sometimes, as a professional, it is tough to separate your ethics from your personal feelings. My conclusion to this case is that greater love had no man who sacrificed everything for the welfare of his family. His love was strong and untainted. He had sacrificed everything to make his marriage a success, but it takes two committed adults working in harmony.

For a miniscule moment, I felt that Jose was a more dedicated father than most Americans. Tears poured from my eyes as I read the documents. I swirled my chair away from Jose to hide my true feelings. Outside my office was the scenic and tranquil Atlantic Ocean compared with the turmoil boiling inside the heart of Jose. My expression was stone-faced. I responded slowly, "Jose, a paternity test is a DNA test that seeks to establish whether the father is the true biological father. They are normally 100 percent accurate. I am sorry, my friend, but the paternity test showed that you are not the biological father."

Jose stared at me with a blank expression like he had seen a ghost. His face turned pale and lifeless. For too long, he was buried in deception and deceit. I could sense the pent-up anger and frustration in his face. He screamed sorrowfully like a wounded animal from the top of his voice. He cuffed the wall very violently. My assistant was so startled that she moved away from him. He started to cry like a newborn baby grasping for the first breath of air. His heart was shattered into a million pieces. Despite, my ALS issues with my weakened legs, I reached out to embrace Jose. I hugged him tightly. He shouted and cried like a dying soul, "My God, my God, why? Why me? I could love my little Jose even though he is not my own flesh and blood. He will still be my baby forever. I will care for him like I have done in the past."

For several minutes, he cried out loudly with his head bowed down. Hugging him made me cry openly. I continued, "I am sorry, my friend, but life is not always fair. Considering this new evidence, you must face reality."

Jose replied firmly, "No, no. Little Jose is mine. He is my baby. I cannot live without him. My son is my life. He is all that I have to live for in America."

I shook Jose violently. "Listen to me. All your anger will only hurt little Jose. If you truly love him, then you will walk away. Maybe one day, he will come back to you. You must let your baby go for his own good."

With my final words, Jose rushed out of my office like a raging bull. However, it was my ethical duty to submit the new evidence to the court. This is one hearing in court I will not want to miss. The presiding judge in the case gave Dr. Maria a harsh tongue-lashing. Was the judge in a bad mood? After reading the new evidence, she literally told Maria's lawyers to shut up and sit down.

She said with confidence, "This case is full of deception and deceit. The court in the past has treated Mr. Jose unfairly. Was it because of his lack of command of the English language? Was there prejudice against him as a refugee? However, considering the new evidence, I am going to prosecute Dr. Maria for being dishonest to the courts with the maximum sentence that the law dictates. Furthermore, she made Jose's life a living hell. Maria's deceitful behavior gets a lot of devoted, responsible, and loving fathers in trouble with the law. The court loves to side with the alligator tears of some mothers. Are some of their concerns genuine? Yes. Dr. Maria, I am assuming that you are a dedicated medical doctor. You knew that Jose was not the biological father of your child, yet you led him to believe otherwise. Men behave like fools when they are in love. Imagine a medical doctor practicing with that state of mind with such vicious treachery and deceit. Your plan borders on criminal intent. You create a malicious reputation for all mothers. As a woman, I am genuinely sorry for your cold heart. A wife brings a warm loving atmosphere to a home."

Her piercing eyes were focused directly on Maria. You could hear a pin drop in the courtroom. She philosophically added but with venom in her words, "Lies are pieces of the truth but full of deceit. Hatred is easy to sell, but true love needs assurance and commitment. The meaning of the words *love* and *mother* goes hand in hand together, an unbreakable bond of love. It is my belief that one day, God and Jose can forgive you for your sins. As a judge, I cannot forgive you. Little Jose is legally your child. Emotions and love are lethal weapons in the wrong hands. As women, we are sometimes guilty of that crafty behavior on our gullible partners. We use sex and our bodies to achieve our goals. It is the court's decision that you pay Jose fifty-six thousand dollars in restitution at once. Failure to pay within one week will result in your immediate incarceration. God will deal with you. Mr. Jose, Sir, you are not the biological father of the child. Therefore, you have no legal rights. I have given you the maximum monetary compensation allowed by the law. Sadly, and with bitter regret, that is my ruling."

Suddenly little Jose shouted, "No! I want my papi. I love him. I love you, Father. I love you. I want my papi."

Dr. Maria, his mother, was surprised at his sorrowful words. With a wave of her hand, the judge motioned the bailiff to take little Jose to his mother. Jose started to cry. He pleaded, "Your honor, I am not rich, but I cannot accept Dr. Maria's money. All I want is custody of my son. Thank you. I love him. I beg you."

The judge answered, "I fully understand your predicament. I am very sorry, but that is not possible. Maria, you will be incarcerated in prison for one month."

Jose immediately bolted out of the courtroom in tears. My mind was totally absorbed in her profound philosophy. Her ruling was justified within the constraints of the law. Jose was never heard from again. Rumors were that he returned to Cuba in search of his family.

After fifty years of futile trade restrictions, President Barack Obama resumed normal relations between USA and Cuba. Donald Trump is now the newly elected President of the United States of America. Dictator Fidel Castro, thankfully, has passed away. Cuban exiles in Miami celebrated his death. In his final days as President, Mr. Obama removed the wet feet, dry feet law. That means that any Cuban trying to make their desperate journey to USA will be deported back to their homeland. It is my hope that one day, the Cuban people can legitimately vote and have a genuine democracy.

Jose felt comforted on his return to his beloved Cuba. He never accepted the blood money as compensation from the court. He always blamed the United States for all the Cuban problems. In our interview, he had told me that Castro made Cuba an island prison for his people, but America's restrictions on trade embargo only hurt the poor Cubans. He cried when Fidel died. Jose had traveled back to Cuba abroad the first cruise ship from the port of Miami. Jose's first stop in Cuba was to his hometown.

Sadly, his Cuban wife had moved on with her life. She had replaced Jose with another Jose occupying his own home. His children were graduate medical doctors working in Africa. Jose was called *Un traidor a la revolucion Cubana* or a traitor to the Cuban revolution. Jose had lost everything. Was his desperate journey worth the agony? Jose started the first Uber taxi service in Havana.

Fast forward 10 years later. Dr. Maria's son, Jose, visited Cuba when he turned eighteen years old. He never returned to Miami. Rumors spread that he had joined the man who really cared for him. The man, he was proud to call his papa.

My mind wondered on relationships and cheating throughout history. There are several accounts in the Bible of Adam and Eve, Samson and Delilah. Cheating is as old as civilization. Now there is even a cheater's hotline. Everyday, politicians answered similar allegations with these words that they never have sex with this woman.

This is a poem on refugees and their ultimate sacrifice by Warsan Shire:

> you have to understand
> that no one puts their children in a boat
> unless the water is safer than the land
> i want to go home,

but home is the mouth of a shark
home is the barrel of a gun
and no one would leave home
unless home chased you to the shore

Refugees are refugees not by choice but by the selfish, uncaring, and indiscriminate actions of the leaders of their countries. When will elected leaders be devoted and caring parents to their people?

CHAPTER FOUR

A Clash Of Cultures:
East Meets The West

The sun was setting in the distant horizon as I drove from the courthouse in Downtown Miami toward Miami International Airport. Recently, there seems to be a continuous traffic congestion plaguing the streets of Miami. Was it because of an ever-increasing immigrant population from the bankrupt countries of Puerto Rico and Venezuela and others in Central and South America? Were their journeys desperate?

From the courthouse in Downtown Miami to the airport took me a mind-blowing two hours. Normally, the same journey takes about half an hour. Then the reason for the delay appeared in front of my eyes. Someone had carelessly driven on the wrong side of the Interstate 95. Their idiotic action led to the loss of five innocent lives. Two cars were literally smashed into little pieces and were on fire. Ambulances, highway patrol, fire rescue, and two medical helicopters were on scene. Were our new cars been made from flimsy materials? For a moment, I thought they were filming a movie. On the other hand, my old SUV smashed into the side railing and only had a little dent. Pieces of both cars were scattered everywhere. Nevertheless, I anxiously approached Miami International Airport.

Krishna, my son, waved his hand as I approached the international arrival area. I discreetly parked in a "no parking" zone and carefully jumped out my van. My legs were numb; they buckled, causing me to fall unto the incoming traffic. Krishna realized what was happening and rushed to my assistance. He hugged me tightly like a shepherd finding his long-lost sheep. He said calmly, "Papa, are you okay?"

I nodded, embarrassed but with a reassuring smile. I hurriedly hopped into the driver's seat when I realized that the traffic police were heading swiftly in my direction. I shouted, "Let's go guys. This is a no parking zone. I will get a ticket."

I started my vehicle and continued driving. Just then, I heard my angel say from the back seat in a voice that was sweet and serene as I recollected. "Papa, how are you? I really missed you. Did you forgot that your little girl was sitting in the back seat? Did you miss your little angel?"

My heart skipped a beat as I extended my hand to touch my baby. Tears filled my eyes. She squeezed my hand. I felt the tender love flowing between a father and daughter again, a special bond that can never be broken, even by a separation for two years. As I glanced at my rearview mirror, I noticed that my daughter's head was covered with a black cloth. I responded inquisitively, "Baby, are you sick? Do you have a high fever? Why is your head covered with a black cloth on a hot, humid day in Miami?"

Krishna looked at me with the answer close to his tongue, but he never answered my questions. In my haste to leave the airport, I did not realize that two people were sitting in the back seat of my banged-up SUV. Lisa, my daughter, calmly said, "Daddy, this is Ahmed, my husband. We were married about eight months ago in the refugee camp in Syria. He is a medical doctor working with volunteers for humanity. His family was killed by terrorists in Syria."

I was traumatized at her firm but gentle words. In my astonishment, my foot instinctively reached for the brakes to slow my vehicle. I stared discreetly into my rearview mirror again and again to get a better view of new son-in-law. I saw a brown-skinned bearded man with a Middle Eastern countenance. I felt betrayed and rightly upset. My tone of language became very sarcastic. I added loudly, "What? When? Are you kidding me? Are you joking? Have you forsaken your parents?"

Krishna was visibly amused by my loud tone. Lisa kept her silence for a few minutes. She managed to wear a half smile. "Papi, I am truly sorry. In Syria, we work twenty-four hours a day. We are occupied with saving people's lives from terrorists' attacks, Russian bombers, and the Syrian army. I am sorry. Anyway, Ahmed is hoping to work and live here in Miami permanently."

My tone of voice changed to be very cynical. "That is so strange. We Skype regularly. You work twenty-four hours a day. However, you find time to get married without revealing such a big decision to your parents. Ahh... grow up, Lisa. I am not that foolish—"

Ahmed interrupted my erratic behavior, "As-Salaam-Alaikum." I looked at him, stone-faced, through my rearview mirror. He clearly saw that I did not understand his statement and quickly added, "Peace be upon you, my dear father. I speak little American. I am sorry that we made you upset."

I added with more venom in my voice, "Don't speak American to me. Just speak English."

Afterwards, there was a deadly silence as we drove homeward. Tension filled my vehicle. The ringing of my cell phone shattered the deadly silence. It was my wife, Anita. She had requested that we meet her at our family restaurant, Krishna and Lisa International Restaurant, for dinner.

Inside, my heart was boiling with anger and betrayal. My frustration and rage were directed solely against my daughter, Lisa. My little girl had betrayed my trust in her. How could she marry one year ago and keep her marriage a secret from her caring parents? Was she embarrassed that she had married outside her culture and Christian beliefs? Did she follow her heart without fully understanding the circumstances of her actions? After all, when you are in love, you want to scream with joy to the entire world. Would Ahmed be capable of adapting to a strange and foreign way of life? Will he compromise his Middle Eastern values and traditions for Western values?

We reached our restaurant after a brief time. Everyone continued their song of silence. As my vehicle approached, Anita rushed to greet us. She hugged Krishna and Lisa with tears streaming from her eyes. There were tears of sadness and loneliness that were pent up inside for two years of solace. Everyone started to cry. Ahmed backed away like a caged lobster. He sensed that this was a private moment for this family that was separated by time and fate. I kept my distance as my wife lovingly embraced her children. Tom and John joined the celebrations. Finally, my family was reunited again.

Anita's father was here. Everyone affectionately called him *Nana*. I affectionately called him *Big Joe*. Anita had many questions in her mind. "My dearest Lisa, why are you wearing a cloth wrapped around your head? Do you have a fever? Are you sick? Who is that man standing behind you? Is he a customer from the restaurant waiting to be served?"

Lisa added proudly, "Mommy, this is my husband, Ahmed. We were married in Syria for a little more than a year. He is a practicing Muslim. He is from Syria. My headwear is called a hijab. It is like a veil. It is worn by Middle Eastern women as a symbol of privacy and good morality. I am very comfortable wearing it. It is a cool wear. Every woman should wear it. I am sorry that we kept our marriage a secret."

Anita froze with a pent-up anger as she tried to digest her daughter's traumatic news. She took a deep breath as she looked with fury into Lisa's eyes. The unexpected news had hit her like a ton of bricks. However, she managed a faint smile. She demanded that her daughter follow her to her office. We were left standing outside her office. We could hear the mother and daughter yelling at each other. Sometimes parents are the last one to know the intimate lives of their amorous children.

After half an hour of what was a friendly interrogation, Anita entered the dining area with a half-smile on her face.

Lisa was visibly shaken by her mother's intense conversation. Her tender hands were trembling, and she was visibly upset. She held unto her husband for moral support.

My wife waved her hand in a nonchalant fashion. We followed her to the dining area. My complete family had gathered together for this reunion. My four children—Tom, John, Lisa, and Krishna—were here. Of course, my ever-caring and jovial father-in-law, Anita's father, was always present.

I knew that my loving wife was raging mad. Anita was an experienced wrestler verbally, a no whole bare woman. She does not easily mince words. Afterwards, we sat to have a scrumptious buffet meal. Ahmed's beaming eyes carefully scrutinized our restaurant's international menu. Ahmed stood up and, with a gentle somber voice, said, "My dear family, I am truly very sorry. I mean no disrespect. Your restaurant serves pork or non-halal meats which are against my religious beliefs. In my holy book, the Quran, Allah strictly forbids his followers to consume pork meat. I am sorry, but my foods are prepared according to my Islamic law."

Anita stood up to address Ahmed. She was literally breathing fire. She screamed, "What the hell do you mean 'no pork'? My restaurant would go bankrupt without pork! America consumes the most amount of pork in the world.

Hispanics love our pork. Everyone loves pork. We call that supply and demand."

Lisa raised her head hysterically. She bluntly said, "Mommy, I am sorry, but I strongly support my husband if he decides not to eat at our restaurant. I am sure we can find some halal, nonpork menu elsewhere. I am his wife. Then I must support him in whatever he decides. By the way, I do not eat pork either." She paused for a moment then continued, "My family, I love you all with all my heart. However, my life has traveled in a new uncharted direction. I was ashamed to tell you all that I had married a foreigner who is a practicing Muslim. I knew that you all will go crazy."

Krishna intervened with a nifty smile, trying to pacify an explosive situation. "My dear sis, you are very funny. Years ago, in this same restaurant, your favorite meat on the menu was pork. You loved the spicy Trinidadian pudding made from pig's blood and intestines. You loved our restaurant's baby back ribs. Sis, I am very surprised and flabbergasted. You love the pig tail soup and pelau. I am a vegetarian. Meat is cooked here. I do not complain, nor do I eat meat. I just select vegetarian dishes. Ahmed, we cannot dictate how other people live their lives. You have the freedom to choose your own path in a nonviolent way. Here in USA, you have freedom of choice. Brother Ahmed, this is America. You must adapt to a change of country, or you will not endure in the United States. Adaptation is the key to your very survival. Ahmed, Brother, leave what you have learned in Syria there. Do not eat pork. However, do not make it an issue or a major problem. Maybe you can order chicken or beef products."

Silence filled the room. How proud can a father be when his son, Krishna, expounded common sense over a volatile situation? Common sense is not inherited from parents. In fact, it is an asset worth more than a university education. He continued, "You wanted to live comfortable in America, then learn their customs and values. Sometimes they are nice or just ridiculous ways to your mind. However, learn to love or work around the ones that you do dislike very discreetly. America is a Christian country. Unlike other parts of the world, the constitution protects any religious beliefs. Freedom to practice whatever you want to worship is every American's God-given right. Americans, unlike other countries in the world, accept all religions with open arms. Ahmed, my brother, maybe you can buy any meat of your choice at your nearby supermarket and cook it at home. Can you cook, Ahmed?" You could feel the tension in the room at Krishna's valid but pointed question.

Ahmed answered arrogantly. "In my culture, women cook and take care of their men. Lisa will cook for me like she did in Syria. My wife will cook halal foods for me."

Anita joked, "Are we talking about the same Lisa? When my daughter left for Syria, she couldn't boil an egg. Can my Lisa cook? My God, miracles do happen. This is good news to my ears."

Lisa answered proudly, "Yes, Mummy. I will cook for my man every day."

I interrupted their conversation. "I know Miami inside out. Daily, I have a craving for a variety of scrumptious food. Finding places that serve halal foods are like finding many needles in a haystack. Honestly, I do not know of any place in Miami that serves your halal foods." I was honestly quite ignorant of Muslim culture. I inquired inquisitively, "What is halal food? I am afraid my knowledge on this topic is very limited or had no knowledge."

My question was pointed directly to Ahmed. He gazed at me then faked a faint smile. Ahmed proudly stood up to answer, "Halal meats are killed in accordance with Islamic law as written in the holy Quran."

My second question followed quickly, "Where in Miami are you going to get halal foods in restaurants or places that do not serve pork?"

Ahmed was taken aback by my direct line of questioning. As a father, I wondered why would Ahmed leave his country and flee to a non-Muslim country without understanding the vast difference in culture that were totally dissimilar and foreign to him? Was he planning to change the system here? Was he totally mesmerized by my daughter's love that he did not look any further? Was my daughter his ticket or pathway to becoming an American citizen? After all, love makes the brain go crazy.

Lisa pushed her chair aside to stand beside her husband. She sensed that everyone was against him. Muslim culture and their beliefs were totally new to my family. We had no Muslim friends but wanted to be informed about their beliefs and traditions. Lisa lovingly held her husband's hand and spoke softly. "Whatever it takes, I will support my husband. We will find halal meats. We will pray five times daily together. I will follow him to the ends of the earth. After all, your daughter is now a converted Muslim. My husband's faith is now my faith. I follow the teachings of Islam reverently and to the ends of this earth with Ahmed."

Anita, my normally talkative wife, was unusually quiet during this conversation. However, she bumped in. "Ahmed, coming to a foreign country can be a heartbreaking experience. I came from a tiny island called Tobago where everyone is very sociable. You knew your neighbors. They shared everything with one another. In America, everyone is not as friendly as our family. When I came to Miami, no one wanted to be my friend. We want to learn about your Middle Eastern culture. America has material possessions abundantly but not a lot of love. Everyone keeps their distance. Ahmed, you cannot come to a foreign country and expect them to change their values. Lisa, my love, since you were a baby, you were taught that the first religion was love. True love is the first religion. Truth and devoted friendship follows closely behind. My husband and I taught our four children that all religions are the same, just different interpretations of God. Faith comes from the heart with love by showing others a caring and loving spirit. Do not be narrow-minded and believe that God likes one set of people and culture more than others. In the eyes of God, everyone is equal. Religion is truly an artificial concept of God. Ahmed and Lisa, you must follow truth and love. That is the pathway to heaven."

Lisa stood up like a raging bull and shouted loudly in defense of her husband, "How dare you all make a mockery of my husband's beliefs or call his beliefs narrow-minded! Mummy, you are lecturing my husband about his beliefs. He is a good man with good values. You know what, Ahmed, we will drive around Miami to find a high-quality restaurant that do not serve pork. Good night."

Anita counterattacked discreetly, "Lisa, what are you talking about? My love, I have never said one negative word about your husband's culture. Do not be so sensitive and thick-skinned."

Nevertheless, Lisa waved her hand and commanded Ahmed to join her. He greeted us, "As-salamu alaykum, and peace be unto you all."

Lisa hastily departed with a vague "good night" and not a smile on her troubled face. Everyone remained quiet and shocked as they hastily departed from our private dining area. Krishna, sensing the tension in the room, jokingly added, "Love makes the heart turn crazy or, in Hindi term, *pagal.*"

His innocent laughter filled the room. I was worried about my daughter's aggressive change of behavior. A once peaceful, fun-loving family reunion had turned into a battleground about petty differing religious beliefs. My motto has always been to each his own beliefs. Thereafter, we sat silently, eating our buffet dinner. Honestly, as a father, I became too upset to eat even though my belly was groaning for food. There is no worse encounter than a verbal battle with your immediate family. Words can cut deep like a two-edged sword. They can leave emotional scars for a lifetime. The feeling of depression sunk deep within my heart. A stranger with diverse religious beliefs was driving a wedge between my normally loving family.

A quote from Suzy Kassem said, "Understanding languages and other cultures builds bridges. It is the fastest way to bring the world closer together and to Truth. Through understanding, people will be able to see their similarities before differences."

I sat helpless. My daughter's heart was festering with a lethal poison called love. In her eyes, she was confused and tormented by a sudden clash of diverse cultures. Since childhood, my children were taught to be respectful and open-minded about other cultures. When that expectation falls short as a parent, you feel the pain and depression.

Anita realized that my heart was not at the dinner table. She reached out and gently massaged my stiff neck. I looked at my wife. "Daddy's little girl has wings now. Our baby has become an independent woman. Is she searching for answers in her new way of life?" I caressed my wife's hand and continued remorsefully, "Yes, our baby is now a mature woman. She is confused about her role in her new life. We must support her."

Anita whispered softly in my ears, "I guess she does not need old nagging parents interfering in her new love. She needs room to breathe and find herself. She is blinded by a contagious disease call love."

I lovingly looked at her. My professional status as a psychiatrist automatically answered, "True, but Lisa needs us more than ever. She needs our support which I will give her until my last breath of life. She is confused and too stubborn to reach out to ask for advice from us. Time will bring her to her senses. She will seek our advice as time goes by. I hope. We cannot afford to lose our only daughter. It is a waiting game. Give her time to breathe."

Anita teasingly said, "Aha. I guess she is just as stubborn like her pigheaded father."

I snickered, "Do not say the word 'pig.' Someone might be offended." My disposition of depression gradually disappeared as Big Joe entered the dining area with an outburst of his incomparable laughter. Krishna clasped his hands and bowed to touch his grandfather's feet reverently. Joe patted his back respectfully in acknowledgment for Krishna's humble action.

His face glowed with love for his ever-caring grandpa and said, "Namaste. I love you, Nana. I missed you. My thoughts and prayers were with you always."

Joe answered proudly, "You are not my handsome grandson. You are my son." Grandpa Joe lovingly blurted out, "But, but where is my little beautiful Lisa?"

No one answered because no one really knew her whereabouts. He was left in the dark about his little Lisa. Merriment filled the room for the rest of the evening. Ahmed and Lisa never returned during the night. I assumed that they were safe or spent the night desperately searching for halal foods. Lisa never answered her cell phone, text, or Twitter messages.

After our dinner, I retired to the comfort of my bed. My doctor had prescribed Ambien tablets for my insomnia. Strangely, I took one tablet because of the turmoil and my depressed state of mind. However, the Ambien tablet gave me nightmares. I woke up in the patio, unadorned naked. Anita laughed loudly when she saw me.

"Are you mooning the sun with your nudity? Anyway, you will certainly get a lot of vitamin D with your naked posture."

I looked at her very muddled. "My love, you are funny. Honestly, I have no recollection as to how I got to our patio. I remembered taking Ambien then going to our bedroom. The next thing, I awoke here on the patio in the nude." I laughed loudly.

My wife was quiet for a moment. She held my hand very tenderly. "Dr. Jonathan, my love, as you may be aware that Ambien is a very dangerous drug. I have read that patients experienced sleepwalking after taking it. In another patient, they woke up after crashing their vehicle under the influence of the drug, fatally injuring others. This was the most tragic defense. It was reported that a wife allegedly murdered her husband in their bedroom. She blamed it on the effects of Ambien. She was given a lighter sentence. Ambien may cause you to get muscle cramps. You were diagnosed with ALS. Therefore, as a doctor and patient, you should avoid taking Ambien. Anyway, Lisa and Ahmed did not return to our home last night."

I was quick to answer, "I am aware that Ambien can be addicting. You know that Lisa weighed heavily on my mind. I am seriously worried about my Lisa. I felt totally depressed last night."

Anita hugged me with a loving passion. We shared the same pain for our children. "My love, Ambien is not the solution for your sleepless condition. I was up all night, also thinking about our family. Lisa is always my favorite child. My heart bleeds for my baby. I remember when she got her first period. She was so excited, but when she got painful menstrual cramps, she said, 'Mommy, I wish I were a boy.' Anyway, our children are adults. We have one another for comfort and support. Our children now have their own lives."

We hugged each other and started to cry. Our lost sheep, Lisa, returned two days later. The heart is a deceitful thing. Sometimes it cannot separate sense from nonsense or logic from illogical. Life goes on regardless of any dreaded circumstances. I was busy in my medical practice with a suicidal patient when I glanced instinctively at the security cameras. There was my little girl, Lisa, with Ahmed coming into my office. My heart palpitated at the sight of my baby girl. My receptionist ushered them into my VIP waiting area. Well, it was more like our kitchen. My staff loves to cook fresh meals. Why do you think yours truly is fat and overweight? Delicious foods at work and at our family restaurant are not necessarily good for your health.

Today, we were overwhelmed with our new patients. Our desperate journey program was proving to be a goldmine. I laughed myself to the bank. It looks like there are more crazy people in the world. Is the increase in prescribing antidepressants medications, especially selective serotonin reuptake inhibitors, the leading culprit for this drastic increase in suicidal occurrences? My opinion as a leading Psychiatrist does not have much weight against powerful drug companies. They only provide treatment, not cures for diseases.

My next patient was an elderly Latina. Sonia was originally from Honduras in Central America. She painstakingly explained to me, "Dr. Cook, my son Carlos made a desperate journey from my beloved Honduras. My country is full of crime, kidnapping, and gang violence. Carlos could not get employment. In 2013, half of the population was living in poverty. Twenty years ago, my family saved enough money to smuggle my son into USA via Mexico. It was dangerous, but it was worth the risk. Our plan was when he became an American, he would apply to bring his family. Our plan worked, and ten years later, he became an American citizen. During that time, my husband was kidnapped. The police never found his body. In Honduras, despite overwhelming poverty, neighbors were friendly and very talkative. Everyone greeted one another with a smile and *hola* or hello. Neighbors loved to share their cooking. We spent hours gossiping every day. Here in America, neighbors keep to themselves." she lamented. "Both my son and his lovely wife are hardworking Americans. One works in the day, the other works in the night. They hardly see each other only on weekends. They are trying to achieve what they call the great American dream. I ask myself every day, is this any way to live? What is a dream without love? They both work long hours and are paid meagerly wages by fast-food restaurants.

Doctor, I am a sickly old woman. My life everyday are cooking, cleaning, and watching television. The media repeats the same boring news and stupid cartoon shows every day. My jail is my son's house within four concrete walls and steel bars on the windows." She screamed loudly, "Dr. Jonathan, I am going crazy! Help me!"

Her loud antics brought the attention of her son Carlos. He knocked on the door and entered my office quickly. We spoke about her dilemma for a long time.

"Doctor," he confided, "my family are poor immigrants. I cannot afford to place her in an assisted-living facility. It is too costly. Just give her some medications to calm her nerves. Living in the United States is expensive. We live from paycheck to paycheck. We have no savings put aside for a rainy day. We depend on Medicaid and Medicare here for government assistance. My mother will have to adjust to living here like other immigrants. Honduras is not a safe place to live. Crime is rampant. I am sorry. We could hardly afford to pay your fees today." With that statement, he quickly ushered her out of my office. He never waited for my opinion.

My office was now officially closed for the day. The evening sun was sinking in the distant Atlantic Ocean. What an awesome sight—so tranquil and peaceful.

Ahmed and my daughter entered my office. They were missing for two days. My reasoning was that they needed time for themselves and to learn for themselves. Lisa rushed to hug me tightly. I remained sitting. Ahmed stretched his hand to greet me. He managed a half smile. With the wave of my hand and a broad smile, I motioned them to be seated on my couch. Lisa laughed heartily like my loving daughter of days gone by. I recollected that she ran through the house, playing and laughing with her family. She started to speak with her radiant smile.

"You know, Daddy, it was very funny. Everyone mistook me for a Hispanic and Ahmed as a Pakistani. My husband was not amused apparently by being called a Paki. We spent all day combing every street in Miami, looking for a restaurant that serves halal food. There was not a single restaurant that served foods prepared accordingly to Muslims standards. Mummy was right. Pork is a very popular meat enjoyed by most Americans regardless of their religious background.

On our second day, we learned our lesson. We were starving, and it was getting very dark. We walked involuntarily into a small inconspicuous restaurant. The people who owned it was of Jewish descent. You are aware, there is an everlasting history of hatred between Arabs and Jews. They have fought countless meaningless wars over petty differences. Those senseless wars were at the expense of millions of innocent lives. Trillions of dollars were squandered away that could have been used to improve the lives of their people. Ahmed hesitantly walked into the small restaurant. We were warmly greeted by the soft welcoming words from an elderly man, *Shalom*. It is a Hebrew word simply meaning, 'I greet you in peace.' The old man smiled and bowed reverently with the popular Arabic words, *Marhabaan*, which we understood. Simply translated, it means 'hello.' It was a small yet cozy family restaurant, nothing fancy but very clean. However, the ambiance was serene and tranquil. Strangely, we felt at home in here. We saw a teenager boy sweeping the floor and happily singing a Hebrew song. An old lady was serving meals to customers who looked like Russian, Polish, and Hungarian. In Syria, we met Russians. They were deeply involved in the Syrian conflict.

During their senseless bombings, a Russian warplane crash-landed, but the female pilot ejected safely. We cared for her until she returned safely to their air base. Anyway, we were famished and tired from the constant walking. At this moment, we could have eaten anything. An elderly Jewish gentleman came to serve us some tea. We told him that we were looking for halal foods. He grinned mockingly to show his missing front teeth. 'I am sorry. We do not serve halal foods, but we do not cook pork. Our menu is kosher in accordance to strict Jewish customs. I serve very healthy and nutritious Jewish meals. Do you see a lot of customers in my restaurant? No, but the few that come return again and again very satisfied. Son, I am an immigrant like you. I escaped the holocaust in Germany during World War II. Adolf Hitler sent millions of my people to the gas chambers or crematoriums alive. I was lucky to escape to America. Survival here is difficult, but there is peace and tolerance between different races. Anyway, many Americans crave for junk food to healthy meals, for example, McDonald's and Wendy's restaurants, which are always jam-packed with customers. To survive, my family are my workforce. My Arab friend, please try our meal. You will like it. I will give you some samples.' The owner of the restaurant, Mr. Beinstein, realized that Ahmed was skeptical to partake in his food. After all, in the Middle East, both Jews and Muslims are sworn enemies for life. His piercing eyes were focused directly on Ahmed in a truly peaceful loving mode. He continued, 'My son, in America, both Jews and Arabs live like brothers. Here in America, Jews and Arabs work side by side to improve or attain peace, goodwill, and harmony. Life is too short to fight. Enjoy it. You know, Ahmed, some of my best friends and patrons are from Arab countries.'

He jokingly added, 'The Jews and Arabs have one thing in common. They do not eat pork. My tasty meals are prepared with love. They are prepared to the highest kosher standards. The Jews traveled to Russia on a desperate journey, seeking sanctuary from the murdering Adolf Hitler. More than two million Soviet Jews died during the holocaust in warfare in Nazi-occupied territories. The Jews are a most hated people, but we are an enduring race.'

Mr. Beinstein brought us some samples of his delicious dishes. He served us a mouthwatering bread called shabbat, along with challah and cholent. Dad, you must taste their cholent. It is a combination of stewed chicken, lamb, vegetables, and beans. Ahmed at first was extremely skeptical to eat the meals of his sworn enemy from the Middle East. However, his hunger pains were traumatizing."

Ahmed blushingly said, "At least, they do not serve pork."

My husband ate enthusiastically or almost ravenously. The old man looked at Ahmed. He managed a half smile then pondered for a minute. 'My friend, leaders teach us to hate other races. They get strength through our disharmony. They feed us fake news through the media. The latter tell us how to think and formulate good or bad opinions of others. My friend, keep an open mind on all issues. The world is one people.' As we departed, he greeted us politely in proper Arabic, 'Wa alaykumu as-salam.' In English, it means 'Good day and peace be unto you.'"

Ahmed interrupted, "I could not comprehend the humility of that Jewish family. As a boy, I was taught that the Jews were my sworn eternal enemies. What was amazing, he could even speak my native language, Arabic, very fluently. As a Muslim, I could not speak one word of Hebrew. I realized that change must come from within me. I must balance carefully my religious beliefs and accept what this wonderful country has to offer me. Father, I love your daughter Lisa with all my heart. I must learn and respect her culture. She is a devout Christian. We must worship as one family in both faiths. This American dream is only possible if we work in harmony as a team."

For a moment, I wanted to hug my son-in-law. I twirled with my pencil then responded, "Ahmed, my son, time is the master of your destiny. Absorb the good and reject the bad. Time and common sense will resolve all your problems." I continued like a nursery child fiddling with my pencil then added, "Marriage is a marathon not a dash of a hundred meters. It requires patience and understanding, especially where cultures are totally different and unique. Adaptation is the key to success. Pride and arrogance will lead to failure. Communication is the key to a successful marriage. There is no GPS to guide you, but you must work your way diligently through every curve or obstacle that comes in your pathway. Certainly, you will make mistakes, but with an open mind, you will find solutions. Do you want to be a good American? You must show love and respect for the American flag. Your personal values are important, but remember, you are married to a Christian woman. You must respect her beliefs. Remember, Ahmed, no one has seen the face of God. The face of God is true love. Love conquers all obstacles."

I paused for a moment to hear my son-in-law's response. Ahmed was quick to answer very proudly, "In my culture, a wife gives up her old values when she is married and follows her husband's teachings. She has no choice in that decision. She blindly follows her husband's path for better or for worse without questioning his strategies for their lives. We follow Sharia law, and that is the only law for me."

There was a deadly silence in the room for a moment. I stood up to defend my America. "Ahmed, my son, this is America. This country is not perfect, but everyone has equal rights. Everyone has equal civil liberties under our laws. Women also have equal rights or, in some cases, more rights than a man. Here, you must let Lisa worship in her own way. The American constitution protects freedom of worship for everyone. They can dress or follow whatever their heart desires. Ahmed, my son, if you want to live happily in America, then you must comprise some of your values. Open your heart to the modern and changing world."

Ahmed stared in my direction like he had seen a ghost. He had lost his tongue. He stammered for words. "In my country, women are not equal to men. They are treated like a piece of merchandise. It is truly a man's world. A man's world is protected by Sharia law."

I quickly added, "Please explain the concept of Sharia law."

Ahmed answered arrogantly, "Sharia law is loosely put as the law of Islam. These laws cannot be transformed. These laws are meant to regulate public and private behavior. These laws are very restrictive and intrusive, especially against women. For example, a Muslim who becomes a non-Muslim is punishable by death. Criticizing Allah, our true God, is punishable by death. Mocking Allah is punishable by death. A man can beat his wife for insubordination without any punishment from the authorities—"

I stopped Ahmed. I had heard enough to make my head spin frantically crazy. Why would my Lisa live under Sharia law? Is she losing her marbles? I heard enough of these ancient laws to be totally dismayed. I simply added, "You are in the United States of America. There is gender equality. You cannot force anyone to get married in this country. Women can decide their future without consent from anyone. Marriage is equality in sharing your achievements, goals, and aspirations. It is called mutual respect and love."

Lisa sat quietly and was totally engrossed in our contrasting versions of life. Did she agree with her husband's opinion? She never uttered a word. Was my daughter a weakling or a strong American woman? Did the overexposure to the cultures of the Middle East control her inner thoughts? It was a long day at my office. My body was drained mentally and physically. I added, "Oh, by the way, my wife hired a Muslim chef to cook halal foods at our restaurant. There will be no pork served in this special dining area. It is a separate and very secluded area away from the main dining rooms. You must try our halal foods tonight. You will love it. Ahmed, you are a lucky guy. My wife has bent head over heels to accommodate your Middle Eastern values."

Lisa was ecstatic. She shouted with excitement, "Thank you, Daddy! You are still the best. Always love you."

She rushed upon me like a rampaging bull to embrace me. My answer was simple. "All credit goes to your mother and your brother John. It was their brilliant idea."

Ahmed was still skeptical. He did not answer. Later that evening, we drove to our restaurant to taste our new halal menu. With numerous media releases, this area of our restaurant was packed to full capacity. From their unusual apparels, I would only conclude that our new customers were from countries like Saudi Arabia, Jordan, Dubai and Kuwait. The men were elegantly dressed in long white robes, and the women wore black, covered from head to toe. My curiosity was on high alert. The menu was different and unique. Iranian dishes were scintillating in taste. Their main dishes were a unique combination of saffron rice with meats or fishes plus vegetables and fruits. Ahmed was pleased to be surrounded by his culture and his people.

Time flew quickly and two years later, Ahmed passed his medical board exam. He was awarded a job at a most prestigious hospital in New York. It was a Jewish corporation. Lisa gave birth to my handsome grandson, Akram. I was ecstatic. Against my better judgment, they decided to move to New York.

Ahmed jokingly said to me, "At least at this Jewish hospital, they do not serve pork. Lisa and I want to try a diverse environment to start our family. Here in Miami, no one understands my style of living. There are hardly halal meats served in restaurants here. New York is more diverse in foods and culture. Honestly, Papa, I need to meet more of my people."

I steered emotionlessly straight into Ahmed. I wondered what the hell he meant by "my people." That statement resonated in the depths of my mind to this day. Who did he consider to be his people? Was my family in the circle of his people? My family certainly treated him like one of our own. Was his phrase "my people" a slip of his tongue, or did my son-in-law felt alienated in a foreign land?

In New York, Ahmed encountered a lot of hate, anger, and psychological pressure from his fellow coworkers about his name and skin complexion. In his absence, they nicknamed him the Taliban kid, towel head, or Paki. He never wore an Arab headgear or turban, yet some Americans childishly associated him with those people. Ahmed thought that Americans were very narrow-minded and bigoted people. His family moved to Brooklyn, New York, in a small area called Little Syria. They lovingly named my grandson *John Akram Mohammed*. Akram in Arabic means "most generous." Ahmed believed that since America was so kindly generous to him, it was wise to honor the country by his son's name. I was honored that my grandson was named after me. John was also the name of our new President Donald John Trump.

The attack on 9/11 on the Twin Towers changed many New Yorkers' perception about Middle Eastern people. Some New Yorkers assumed that Middle Easterners were terrorists. Nevertheless, Ahmed kept on providing respectable professional health care to his patients. The average American was fearful of the words "Allah aur Ackbar" or "God is great." He said it but silently. He shaved his beard completely. At the hospital, Ahmed left the door open to reassure his patients that he was not a threat to their well-being. Ahmed kept his Muslim values close to his heart. He suffered in silence and told no one, not even to his faithful wife, Lisa. Still, he attended Catholic mass occasionally with his wife and son.

Young Ahmed was admired by all. His unique blue-green eyes were a source of admiration on his handsome face. Lisa told Ahmed jokingly, "Our son will have many female admirers. He will break many hearts."

At the mosque, his friends discussed about being governed by Sharia law. Almost 30 percent of American Muslims surveyed have faith in their legitimate right to be governed by Sharia laws. But why Ahmed contemplate? We already have American laws, and we live in America. The United States of America had civil rights for all their citizens enshrined in the constitutions. Equality to all. Their citizens had true freedom. He saw countries with Sharia law beheading its citizens on the public streets. Facebook and YouTube featured these barbaric acts repeatedly. He believed that after 9/11, New Yorkers viewed Middle Eastern people with a high degree of fear and trepidation. This included people from the Caribbean who had never been to the Middle East, especially those of East Indian descent.

Lisa also sensed that aggressive change in attitude—a changing tide—after their city was viciously attacked. At the New York hospital where Lisa worked as a nurse practitioner, her friend sarcastically asked her one day, "As a proud American, how do you like being married to a Muslim man?"

Lisa was visibly offended by her remark but answered politely, "I have never been loved and respected more in my life. He treats me like a princess and is a good father to our son. My home is heaven on Earth." Her colleague was in a state of shock at her sincere answer. Lisa coerced Ahmed to return to Florida.

I was proud of my Muslim son-in-law. He had achieved the American dream yet retained his Muslim values. I was beginning to see what fascinated my daughter to love this man. She told me confidentially a few details about her husband as a Good Samaritan in New York.

"What is a Samaritan?" I inquired.

She explained, "In ancient Israel, in the dialects of Aramaic, a Good Samaritan was a compassionate and selfless person who helped people in distress. Ahmed had performed many surgical procedures at no cost to many patients. Every Friday, after prayers in the mosque, he walked through Central Park and fed the homeless. He is a humble man. That is why I love him. He never boasted about anything and puts his family first and foremost in his life. I get angry with him in my mood swings, but he just smiles."

On his return from New York, he sat alone and unannounced patiently, waiting at my reception area. He said, "Papa, I have a proposal for your ALS issues. My medical team has developed a new and innovative state-of-the-art procedure for treating ALS involving stem cell. What basically transpires, we harvest adipose tissue from your abdominal area or your bone marrow. My team of doctors extracts your stem cells using new state-of-the-art methods. These new cells are injected into your spinal cord to help fight your ALS symptoms. Then you take some hyperbaric oxygen treatment. As you are totally aware, Papa, that no medical procedure has a 100 percent guarantee of complete success. I am not a gambling man, but is it worth a try? My medical team has had fantastic results in New York. Some patients call our surgical procedure a miracle of modern science."

Without a second thought, I blurted out, "Okay, my son. Let us do it. After all, I have nothing to lose and everything to gain."

Ahmed smiled as he held my hand. He looked straight into my eyes. "Papa, this is my family gift to you. This surgical procedure will not cost you a cent from your pocket. This is my token of appreciation and love to you as my father-in-law. Lisa, Akram, and I love you with all my heart. You've been a very cool and easygoing father. Your family are my people."

For a moment, I embraced him tightly, saying an emotional "Thank you, my son. God bless you. Thank you. I love you."

Tears poured from my eyes as I waved farewell to him. Dr. Ahmed hurriedly departed for Orlando on a cold, windy, and rainy night. He had no choice, but it was very important that he reached his destination on time. The following day, he was scheduled to give an important surgical demonstration on his new and state-of-the art stem cell procedure for neurologists, especially for their ALS and multiple sclerosis patients. Ahmed was excited; he was making an important contribution to his adopted country.

Traveling along US 27 on a rainy and windy day was not a sensible decision. Nevertheless, this route was very familiar to him. After all, he seldom traveled on the Florida Turnpike even though the distance was less in terms of mileage. He laughed out loudly when he thought that Turnpike was full of irrational drivers. On many occasions, his family loved the scenic and tranquil drive along the US 27 to Disney World.

Ahmed was distracted by an incoming text from his wife, Lisa. He focused on reading the contents which read, "Baby, I am really sorry that we missed your departure. There was extreme thunder and lightning. Therefore, we were delayed. On Sunday night, I will make it up to you. Akram wanted to see you before you departed for Orlando. Please do not text and drive. Ha. Lol. Keep your eyes on the road. Your love always, Lisa."

For a few moments, Ahmed was completely engrossed with reading the inbound text. His car swerved helplessly into the crocodile-infested waters. His car began to sink rapidly. Then he screamed loudly, "My goodness! I cannot swim."

He swiftly jumped out his car and held onto a tree branch, fearing for his life. It was pitch-dark, but with every strike of lightning, the sky was on fire. Ahmed saw many pairs of inquisitive eyes frantically moving in his direction.

With fear and trepidation, his body was energized to reach the roadway. His body trembled with horror as his car leisurely disappeared into the murky waters. The fear of dying alone engulfed every fiber in his body as he scrambled to reach the roadway. The frequent flashes of lightning lit up the ominous starless skies, followed by a successive deadly rumble of thunder.

As Ahmed heard the thunderous booming sounds, it brought back horrific memories of Russian MiG warplanes on bombing missions over a helpless Syrian civilian population. He remembered with horror his family's home destroyed in the airstrike. With hands raised to the heavens, he cried out aloud in Arabic, "My God, my God! Allah! Have you forsaken me? Please save my life for Lisa and Ahmed's sake."

The angry bellowing sounds were coming closer and closer near him. He ran instinctively in the opposite direction. From the Animal Planet shows on television, he knew that crocodiles were the ones making that bellowing sounds during their mating season. During this time, they are extremely dangerous, totally aggressive, and very protective of their nests at all cost.

Ahmed was short of breath, and then he realized that when his wife invited him to the gym, he should have accepted her many invitations. His excuses were many and lighthearted, such as "Darling, I have a headache" or "I need to study for a test" or "Your delicious cooking had me upset." As he stopped in the middle of the roadway, he realized that there were two gigantic crocodiles lurking a few feet away from him. He ran as quickly in the opposite direction as his short athletic legs will carry him. By some miracle, Ahmed saw bright lights coming in his direction very frantically. He ran toward the approaching lights, waving and shouting on the top of his voice. The big wheeler stopped abruptly about a hundred feet in front of him. Repeated gunshots rang out near his feet. As Ahmed turned to run, he stumbled on top of two massive bleeding crocodiles. Blood covered his rain-drenched clothes.

He stopped as a hoarse voice in a thick Texan accent loudly said, "I am here to help, my brother. You are safe now. Jesus sent me to save you, brother."

Thereafter, Ahmed found a genuine Christian American friend in Mike Bush. After his nightmarish ordeal, Bush gave him new clothing to attend his medical conference. Nonetheless, he was dressed like an American cowboy. Fast forward into the future, their friendship would be binding for life. They would spend weekends exchanging philosophies about life, religion, and culture. Two years later, Ahmed would travel to Houston, Texas, to perform a lifesaving emergency surgery on his new friend, Bush.

Later, when Hurricane Harvey mercilessly pounded Texas with ferocious high winds and six feet of rainwater, Ahmed would lead a volunteer medical team to their ravage state. They carried a banner that read, "From Florida with love." His wife Lisa, along with the Red Cross, provided medical assistance to all Texans. Anita and I volunteered as babysitters to our loving yet talkative and mischievous grandson Akram while his parents were occupied in Texas. Bush lost everything in the aftermath of Hurricane Harvey. Ahmed stayed in Texas until his friend had rebuilt his life. A few months later, Hurricane Irma hammered Florida mercilessly. During the aftermath, Bush and his friends hurriedly drove from Texas to Miami, bringing an fleet of eighteen-wheelers with much needed emergency supplies.

Now, at present in Orlando, Bush escorted Ahmed directly to his conference. Ahmed arrived late in Orlando, half an hour after his scheduled appointment. His body had a revolting odor of stagnant swamp water. Ahmed was totally exhausted and sleepy from his overnight ordeal. How often do you see a medical doctor of Middle Eastern descent dressed like a Texan cowboy as a guest speaker at an important medical conference?

Dr. Maria was in attendance as an intern neurologist. She had ended her relationship with her American boyfriend after she found him stark naked in her apartment with a blonde doctor. When Dr. Maria entered her bedroom unannounced, her boyfriend's lover was securely handcuffed to her bedpost. In his defense, Maria's amorous lover had told her that his blonde companion wanted to commit suicide. Therefore, he handcuffed her to the bed. While in prison serving her short-term sentence, Maria's boyfriend never came to visit her. After her betrayal, Maria searched frantically for Jose but without any success.

In Hialeah, Jose's former landlord informed her that Jose had returned to Cuba in search of his family. In prison, she realized that Jose was her only devoted friend. She had betrayed a true companion and her soul mate. She kept muttering silently, "Jose, I am sorry. Please forgive me. You are my true love. I am sorry. Please come back to me."

Nevertheless, she realized that it was too late to mend their broken relationship. In her anguish, Maria decided to relocate from Miami to Orlando along with her son to avoid undue emotional stress with her American lover. She wanted to start a new life in a serene and peaceful environment. She reckoned that Orlando was an ideal and fun-loving place for her son.

After Ahmed's conference, his next assignment was a medical demonstration at a nearby private hospital. His stem cell procedure in the operating room was interrupted by a code red alert. Suddenly, a panic-stricken nurse entered the theater with a bloodstained outfit. She screamed, "We have a critical situation in the emergency room! There was a massive shooting at a gay club. Casualties are coming by the busloads. All doctors and nurses are needed in the emergency room immediately!"

Ahmed and Maria rushed to emergency room. Then he remembered that his family members, John and Tom, were partying at a popular gay club in the immediate area. At Tom's repeated requests, they were celebrating John's birthday. Ahmed was invited to the celebrations, but he said that he was not into this gay thing. Ahmed remembered John jokingly saying to Tom, "Brother, I am not gay, but we will celebrate at a club of your choice. My question is what will happen to my straight image?"

John, after much teasing, decided to accompany his brother. Tom answered with a sense of humor, "Brother, remember, I am happy and gay, but that is not my contention. Gay clubs welcome everyone. Lots of bisexual people and lesbians go to parties at gay clubs. My brother, this club is for everyone. Straight and not so straight are all welcome."

On reaching the emergency room, Maria screamed hysterically on observing the mass slaughter of innocent partygoers. Ahmed, on the other hand, was immune to human suffering. On numerous occasions, he had witnessed the slaughter of innocent refugees in his homeland, Syria.

The emergency room looked like a dreadful scene taken out of a horror movie. Ahmed took a deep breath as he placed his trembling hands on his chest. For a split second, he whispered prayerfully, "Allah aur Ackbar, help me. Give me the strength and courage to save these dying innocent souls."

Ahmed worked swiftly and professionally. Those with severe and life-threatening wounds were given priority treatment. The dead were left on the bloody corridors. The smell of death was everywhere. In the name of God, how can anyone justify this horrendous act? Evil is everywhere.

Suddenly, he heard a familiar innocent voice with a grief-stricken cry, "Brother Ahmed, please help us."

The bloody figure lurched uncontrollably in his direction. Those frightful words resonated throughout the hospital corridors. He was frozen in time for a fleeting moment. As he raised his weary head, tears poured uncontrollably from his sleepy eyes. His nightmares in Syria were now a blunted reality in Orlando. Dr. Maria rushed to Ahmed's side. "Doctor, do not be emotional at this time. Your medical experience is desperately needed at this moment. Man, get hold of yourself. Remember, your patients need you."

Dr. Tom was bleeding profusely from massive gunshot wounds to his abdominal areas. Part of his intestines could be seen with the naked eye. Ahmed rushed to his side. He recoiled for a moment as he saw the large gaping wound. Ahmed forgot his exhaustion. He said calmly, "Tom, place this gauge tightly over the wound. Help is here. Where is your brother John?"

Tom started to scream hysterically. With blood gushing from his abdomen and with his bloodstains and trembling hands, Tom pulled Ahmed closer to him and answered very slowly in excruciating pain. "John shielded me with his body when bullets were flying in every direction. The shooter was only a few feet away from our table. He shouted, 'Allah aur Ackbar!' With loaded automatic weapons in both hands, I saw an uncontrollable rage, anger, and hatred in his frightened eyes. He fired indiscriminately in any direction at everyone. My God, as a practicing Psychiatrist, I have never seen such pent-up animal like rage in someone's face. My brother is dead. He was my savior."

With those terrifying words, Tom fainted and slumped to the floor in an unconscious state. He was rushed immediately to surgery. Tom remained in the intensive care unit in an unconscious state for three days. This latest attack was the deadliest mass shooting in USA history. America was again in a state of mourning for another heinous, senseless attack on innocent gay club goers.

Later that night, Ahmed, my son-in-law, called me and my wife Anita to inform us of the tragic demise of our beloved adopted son, John. How do I comprehend this tragic news of my beloved son? As a caring father, I felt like taking my gun and emptying the magazine on the perpetrator of this heinous act. Would that resolve the issue? After all, the Bible declares that an eye for an eye and a tooth for a tooth. However, as a practicing Psychiatrist, the authorities will deal with the issue. Tom was hospitalized for three weeks, undergoing multiple surgeries. Krishna spent every day by his brother's bedside. John was cremated, and his ashes were thrown in his favorite leisure area, South Beach.

Tom spoke mournfully from his heart at John's funeral. "John knew the true meaning of the word *brother*. He sheltered me from this cruel world when the word 'gay' was a social crime. When I secretly confided in John that I was gay, he made fun of me and said, '*Gay* means 'happy.' Are you happy that you are gay? If you are gay and happy, I am happy for you. Gay or not, you are still my loving brother. We must support each other. After all, we are family first and foremost.' When my parents abandoned us, my big brother was my support and strength. He always placed my happiness first and foremost in his life. In college, John was my first defense against numerous bullies. Greater love had no man that he gave his life to save me. As brothers, we had a problematic life growing up. My big brother was never discouraged by any obstacle. He always had a comforting and reassuring smile, always saying, 'Don't worry. Be happy.' He was always there for me even to the end of his world. He shielded me from a barrage of bullets directed at me. We were only a few feet away from our attacker. John threw me violently away from the line of gunfire. Is there life after death? Maybe. God bless you, my brother. In my heart, I know you are looking after me even after death. One day, our paths will meet again. You taught me what true brotherly love meant by your unselfish actions. Love conquers all. I love you, my brother. Our life's journey is not complete. One day, our paths will meet again."

I sat there, speechless and motionless. Another innocent bystander was mowed down by a senseless gun-related violence. John was incredibly strong, but he never hurt a fly. For many years, I had pleaded at numerous medical conferences that gun owners must all undertake a strict and periodic psychiatric evaluation before purchasing a gun. My pleads fell on deaf ears in the medical community. Money talks and bullshit walks. I felt like cursing everyone in my medical community and politicians. You need to be twenty-one years of age to buy a pack of cigarettes. However, to buy a military-style AR assault rifle, you only need to be eighteen years old with no mental evaluation. The law is an ass written by money greedy politicians in the interest of gun manufacturers. I knew that schools would be easy targets for the so-called mentally deranged lunatics. School children are our future leaders yet security at schools are not a priority. It is ironic that every time a politician is seen in public, they are surrounded by heavily armed security police. Why not our schools?

I knelt and cried like a baby. My soul and spirit were torn from my bleeding heart. Anita wept without stopping. She refused my comforting embrace. Her father, Papa Joe, calmly said to me, "Leave her alone. Only time heals this type of wound."

Nana gently placed his hands on the shoulders of his daughter Anita. Our eldest son John, her working partner and comforter, was no more in her loving arms. John and his mom, Anita had taken Krishna and Lisa International Restaurant to a high pinnacle of success. The mother and son team had sacrificed all their time at the restaurant. John's life was at the restaurant. The bullets at close range had disfigured John's body. Krishna advised a close coffin and his remains to be cremated.

At the funeral service, Anita stared, motionless, near John's lifeless body. I was lost for words. John believed in nonviolence but became a victim of the gun. His loving words resonated in my ears: "Daddy, I am lover not a fighter. I love all women."

My adopted son was strong as an ox but meek as a lamb. Dr. Ahmed stepped up toward the coffin. With tears in his eyes, he said, "O Allah, please forgive our brother John as he enters your presence. Exchange his home for a new home. Admit him into the heavenly garden and protect him. Until we meet again, my brother." He placed a single red rose on the coffin.

Krishna prayed next for the departed soul. He quoted a Native American prayer, "Our rites for the dead are meant to help on their journey into the afterlife. Death for us is a vital tool in the cycle of life. Death is a new beginning of life. So, live your life that the fear of death can never enter your heart. Trouble no one about their religion. Respect others in their views, and demand that they respect yours. Love your life, perfect your life, beautify all things in your life. Sing your death song and die like a hero going home. Om Shanti. Let there be peace."

My innermost feelings on the innocent slaughter on my son were simple. Dying for a brave cause is heroic but dying for nothing is senseless. In my heart, I could sense that mass killings by unhinged gun owners were a new terror in our world. Our lives would not be the same again after John's demise. Our lives were thrown in deep mayhem. Anita and Tom went into deep depression. After many hours of nagging and verbal abuse from my wife, I reluctantly prescribed the popular antidepressant medication called Prozac for the both, Tom and Anita. I seriously warned them that this drug may increase suicidal tendencies.

After taking the medication, my ever-smiling Tom was not smiling again. He locked himself in his room. He never spoke to anyone. In his heart, he blamed himself for his brother's death in Orlando. Immediately after taking Prozac, Tom developed flu-like symptoms. He did not tell anyone. Blisters followed by Stevens-Johnson syndrome, a rare disorder of this drug, which were eating his body from inside. Dr. Tom increased his workload with his patients. He extended his working hours late into the night. One day, Tom's lifeless body was found in his office. His head lay face down on his open laptop. My loving son, friend, comforter, and partner was no more in this life. Words could not come out of my mouth. There was a note on his desktop: "My loving parents, I am truly sorry. I love you with all my heart. John, my brother, I am coming home to be united with you in life and in death."

Within one month, I had two funerals for my sons. What can be more tragic than burying your children? Time will never heal the traumas that my family experienced in such a brief time. At Tom's funeral, my grandson, Akram tenderly held my hand. He looked innocently into my teary eyes. His words were soft and tender. "Grandpa, in my dream last night, I saw Uncle Tom and Uncle John. They were very happy. They were talking and laughing with God. I really saw them, Grandpa. I saw them. I saw them for real. Grandpa, are you going to leave me one day soon? Who will play with me and sing with me?"

His childlike, sincere words touched the bottom of my bleeding and broken heart. I knelt to reach his short height. Tears poured from our eyes. Akram hugged me tightly. I said tenderly to him, "My son, Grandpa never dies. They only grow old, and they sleep forever deep your heart. When you think of Grandpa, always smile because he is thinking about you. I love you. My precious little one, Grandpa cannot promise to love you the rest of your life, but I can promise to love you the rest of my life."

We hugged and cried for a moment. His words were precious, serene, and sincere. His touching words brought peace and tranquility to my troubled heart, a peace that surpasses all understanding. Does our journey in life end at death? Is there a journey into the afterlife?

CHAPTER FIVE

A Journey Into the Afterlife: Is it Real?

Time heals all wounds—no. The scars of my sons' demise have left deep scars. After our two sons' untimely death, Anita became completely focused on our restaurant. We became strangers sleeping in the same bed. My normal everyday jovial conversations with her were misconstrued for evil or malicious intentions. My legs, after my stem cell procedure, were becoming stronger, so I hoped for the best. One day, I decided to invite my wife to the gym. I said zestfully, "Anita, baby, I am going to the gym and sauna. Do you want to come with me?"

She blurted out loudly with venom in her voice, "So now you think that I am fat and lazy! I am not beautiful and sexy like the girls in your office. Why did you mention sauna? Do you think that I have an unpleasant body odor?"

That was funny. I started to laugh loudly. My laughter compounded her anger. Anita looked very irritated at me.

She continued, "I am not one of your crazy-ass patients that you can psychoanalyze."

My laughter was stifled, but I thought that her answer was funny. I blurted out, "My love, that is not what I really meant to say. I am sorry." Many years ago, my wise father said that if you want to remain married and be happy, then you need to apologize for everything, even the errors of your partners. As my father told me jokingly, "Women are never wrong." Always say the golden words, "I am sorry."

After my sincere request for forgiveness, Anita rushed out of our bedroom like a raging bull. Was it her postmenopausal behavior or pent-up rage after the death of our sons? Anita did not want or have a conversation about this topic. She suffered in silence. Talking about problems is a stress reliever. Is there a journey after death? What happened to my sons after death? Is *rebirth* a myth? My inquisitive mind carried me to reading about different concepts about the afterlife as well as visits to numerous ashrams, temples, mosques, and churches throughout Florida.

Two things were certain in our life. First, we are born from nothing, and second, we depart with nothing. Well, there is a third dimension that is inevitable. The third one is that we must pay our taxes. My research journey included every major religious belief and culture. I will summarize my acquired knowledge for my ardent readers. This is not your author's opinion. Readers, please come up with your own conclusion.

> The Holy Bible records vividly that Lord Jesus Christ rose from his grave after his death by crucifixion. He ascended to heaven. The Eastern Orthodox Church teaches that three people from the Bible were taken in their physical bodies into Heaven: Elijah, Virgin Mary, and Lord Jesus.

Islamic teachings states that Muhammad ascended into heaven alive at the site of the Dome of the Rock. Muslims believe that Jesus was not crucified, but instead, he was risen by God unto the heavens.

> In Hindu scriptures, death is a wrong word to be associated with the avatars of Lord Vishnu. Their sole purpose is to establish Dharma, and once it is restored, they return to their heavenly abode.

> On the other hand, Islamic doctrine holds that human existence continues after the death of the human body in the form of spiritual and physical resurrection. The afterlife will be one of rewards and punishments that commensurate with earthly conduct. The bliss of the people of

paradise shall never end, and the punishment of unbelievers condemned to hell shall never cease.

Hinduism believes in the rebirth and reincarnation of souls. The souls are immortal and imperishable. A soul is a part of a jiva, the limited being, who is subject to the impurities of attachment, delusion, and laws of karma. Death is not a great calamity but a natural process. Unless the soul is liberated, neither life nor afterlife is permanent. The soul needs to be born again and again until it overcomes its state of delusion, achieves the state of equanimity, and realizes its completeness. Hindus believe in cremating their dead. There are five elements that make up the physical body. Interestingly though, Hindus believe in the existence of ghosts and spirits. The Upanishads refer to stories about ghosts, spirits, and celestial beings possessing human bodies and speaking through them. They are unfortunate souls who, because of a curse or the terrible sins—such as suicide—committed by them, remain suspended in the region between the higher worlds and the earth. They usually seek and trouble people of impure minds and unclean habits.

My mind was blown by this new-acquired information. I was ecstatic in cloud nine. My sons were alive in a different dimension in life and time. Armed with all this fantastic information, I know that one day for certain, Tom and John will be reunited with me after death.

However, there were lingering doubts in my mind. My eldest son, Krishna, was very knowledgeable about the afterlife. I had an unspoken love or a hidden admiration for my eldest son, Krishna. Why? My ardent readers would surely ask, "Why him?"

First and foremost, let me reiterate, I love all my children equally. Do not think for one second that there is an inequity in my love for my children even after death. I call Krishna my no-problem child. My zealous readers, I am sure that you have a child among your immediate family whom you cling closer to your heart. Krishna has always been that self-confident child. There was never a problem that he could not resolve on his own accord. Is it because he is too smart not to get married? He jokingly said that marriage is the main cause for divorce.

Krishna wears his self-confident, utopic smile regardless of any dreaded circumstances. Anita and I, as his parents, do not have his tranquil temperament. His relaxed, tranquil smile and his natural sense of humor make him attractive inside out. He has a lot of female admirers but is not committed to anyone. He is an independent worldwide traveler. Nevertheless, I labeled him my nomadic son. He often reminded me that he was a humble servant of the world. Krishna has crisscrossed the globe, helping refugees in every turbulent and hostile situation. Unlike yours truly, Krishna was not interested in acquiring material wealth or worldly treasures. My son worked diligently to save his money. His ideas and philosophies were different from anyone in my vast field of practice in psychiatry.

Indeed, my Krishna graduated with honors in nursing. It is my opinion that his degree in nursing was to shut up his parents from nagging him to get a job or to have a tertiary education. Nevertheless, Krishna's life was dedicated to making the world a utopic place. He told me, "Papa, the world is one nation. There are no borders for suffering. Despite our difference in color and race, everyone bleeds the same color. The true color of a person is actions from the heart. All the world's population have a refugee connection. We are brothers and sisters in one small world. God created the world as one people without borders. Man created those artificial boundaries."

On reaching Krishna's home, there no parking for my vehicle. His antique beat-up Ford truck and a new Mercedes sports car had totally occupied his parking area.

A stark contrast of the ancient and modern vehicle parked alongside each other.

I took a dangerous and yet stupid chance by parking behind both cars, thereby completely blocking the sidewalk. Inside his home, my son greeted me with his usual utopic and radiant smile. With clasped hands to his chest, he bowed and touched my feet and said the word *namaste*. He explained the meaning of his spoken word. "My soul honors your soul. I honor the place in you where the entire universe resides. I honor the light, love, truth, beauty, and peace within you because it is also within me. In sharing these things, we are united. We are the same. We are one with God and the universe."

So profound philosophy, I honestly wondered if my son was smoking marijuana. He reminded me that the whole world was his family. His thoughts and actions were that of a selfless man walking this planet earth. Since returning from Syria, we had hardly spent father-and-son quality time. Touching the feet of someone was humility, total submission, love, and respect. My heart palpitated as Dr. Maria greeted me with a kiss as she exited from his bedroom. During our discussions throughout the night, my son mentioned that Jesus Christ touched and washed the feet of his disciples. In Hindu philosophy, Lord Hanuman frequently bowed and touched the feet of Lord Rama. We sat for the first time after John and Tom's funeral to tête-à-tête in the quietness of the star-filled night. However, as a concerned parent, I wondered what role Dr. Maria played in my son's life—friends, lovers, or friends with benefits? I remembered vividly how Maria intentionally screwed up Jose's life without any remorse or repentance for her selfish actions.

My curiosity was getting the better of me. Krishna offered us chia tea. We gladly accepted. He hurriedly proceeded to his kitchen. I whispered discreetly, "Maria, how do you know my Krishna?"

She smiled very seductively and responded, "I was working at the hospital that your sons were admitted in the emergency room in the Orlando massacre. I worked with your son-in-law, Ahmed, desperately trying to save the injured ones. I met Krishna while he cared for Tom who was badly injured in the bloodbath. Your son Krishna never left his brother's bedside, except to use the bathroom. I think your question is… Am I intimately involved with your son? I tried, but your son was not interested in me. Honestly, I am looking for a good Hispanic man who understands my culture. There was once a man called Jose who cared and loved me like that love I see emanating from the soul of your son. Jose had said to me one day with a red rose in his hand, 'You are my temple, my prayer, and my angel. You are the reason that I breathe.' I laughed mockingly and said to him, 'Go screw yourself.' Jose looked disappointed at my answer. I used Jose to finance my education. His money was our money. My money was mine. Female Scrooge could be my nickname. My ex-husband Jose paid for everything in our relationship. I controlled and used Jose like a helpless robot or like a puppet on a string. When I barked, he followed my orders.

Today, I am remorseful for my selfish act. I behaved like a real bitch. As a woman and a wife, I used sex like a two-edged sword with Jose to have my way. My true love was a rich American doctor. He was young, handsome, filthy rich, and the bright lights of materialism blinded me from the reality of life. I was deceived by his wealth. I screwed up a good man's life until it was too late. Jose cared for my child like a real man. He showered us with extravagant gifts even though his income was meager. My ex-husband wore the same dress pants and track shoes on every occasion. On the other hand, I never wore a dress more than once or two times. My Gringo lover that I revered and admired was a player, a Romeo and a Don Juan. I was his sidekick. Later, a friend showed me a photo on Facebook of his sexy wife and two children, yet we remained in an intimate relationship. His marriage was of no consequence to me. From our clandestine relationship, I contracted genital herpes from him. My gosh, there was a sensual passion for my American lover that Jose could not satisfy in me. Anyway, antidepressant medications are not helping. In fact, they enhanced my suicidal feelings even more, but I wondered what will happen to my only child."

Maria was talking like she had verbal diarrhea. I wanted to add my miniscule opinion to this interesting conversation since I was well acquainted with her divorced partner, Jose. I quipped in a whisper, "My dear, why do you want another Hispanic man when both men of your culture screwed up your life? Spread your eyes on love. Maybe chose a yellow, black, or a brown person. You know what they say? When you choose brown or black, then the other colors are not important." My son finally returned with his spicy chia tea in a serving tray. He brought four cups of tea. Was he expecting another guest?

Krishna smiled broadly as he gave his homemade brew tea to his guests. There was a gentle knock on the front door. He rushed to answer it. My son-in-law, Ahmed, entered as our third guest. That resolves the mystery of the fourth cup of tea. Ahmed has always been a man of few words. He greeted my frail body with a robust bear hug.

We sat in awe on the patio under the star-filled sky. Krishna's eyes were fixed at the celestial bodies like he was searching for someone in the distance. His mind was focused in the great beyond. He started thoughtfully, "You know, Papa, the vast mysteries of this mystic universe are beyond the human understanding. Man's journey through this vast universe is like a grain of sand in the vast Sahara Desert. Like that grain of sand, he is ignorant of the fantastic mysteries of this complex universe that we call home. Mankind is full of greed, yet he sacrifices his health to accumulate vast wealth. Then, he sacrifices his money to recuperate his health. Then, he is so anxious about the future that he does not enjoy the present, the end result being that he does not live to enjoy the past, present, or future. He lives as if he is never going to die. Throughout my travels, man has this strong passion for accumulating wealth, yet he does not enjoy life. Why?"

I thought, I was invited to answer his question, but my son kept on speaking as he stared lost in the celestial bodies. "Man, by nature is a selfish predator. He has a big ego and generally does not share his possessions, even to his close relations or his loved ones. He is like the ego beaver. This is what makes the refugee crisis. War is big business for wealthy countries. In one hand, they sell guns to opposing enemies, then they provide food and shelter to those affected by the wars."

Krishna smiled at the celestial stars. He continued, "Have you all ever wondered what is the purpose of our lives as we endure on our desperate uncertain journey called life? Have we journeyed through this life before? Is this the sole purpose of our existence to live and then die?"

Was Krishna looking at his ill-informed guests for some answers? We all looked more baffled and confused. As medical doctors, our sole purpose was keeping patients alive. After death was burial, and we knew nothing about the afterlife. Krishna continued, "When a rich man dies, someone else steps in his shoes and enjoys his hoarded wealth. For a widower, some other man enjoys her husband's wealth. The widower will tell her new lover, 'Baby, do not work tirelessly. Enjoy life. Relax. Let me give you a massage. Let me prepare you a hot meal. Remember my no-good hopeless husband never spent time with me. We deserve a long vacation.' Oh, that was meant to be funny. People take life too serious. We must smile and laugh at life. A good smile costs nothing. A frown causes high blood pressure and nervous disorders. As a young man, I have seen so much suffering in the world. It is unbelievable. Man's inhumanity crosses race, religion, and borders. I will tell you why, Papa. Everyone is narrow-minded and disrespectful. We must learn and respect one another traditions that sometimes defy logic.

I will give you an illogical story. An American man was placing flowers on his wife's graveside. He saw a Chinese man placing rice near a grave. The American man saw this as an opportunity to ridicule the oriental man's culture. He shouted scornfully, 'Hey, pal! Do you honestly think that the dead will certainly come back and eat the rice?' The

Chinese was quiet for a moment. He smiled and answered jokingly, "Yes, she will when yours come to smell their flowers first.' Understanding and appreciating diversity in culture unites a country. A simple solution for peace and harmony is unconditional respect and acceptance of one another strange and diverse teachings. That will never happen, but with that acceptance, we will have heaven on earth. When, I clasped my hands, bow, and say, 'Namaste,' it means that I respect your faith and bow to that eternal God living in you. Religion strives for world domination whether through conversion or with the sword."

I was totally impressed with my beloved son's philosophy of life. It was so simple yet profound. I wanted to hear more from his travels. He continued, "This journey in life is not only physical but mental and spiritual. Your body must be harmonized to combine all three elements to attain peace within you. You can journey from country to country, but if there is no inward harmony, peace and love will never be achieved totally. I quote from AnitaPoems.com on world peace. It says,

> When wars and conflicts totally cease,
> In our world, there shall be peace.
> People must learn to get along,
> Not blame others, for being wrong.

They fight for control, fight for land,
Some just need a helping hand.
We should fight for peace instead,
Love not war, we should spread.

The weather was changing to a cold, windy night as I struggled to get on my feet and move closer to my son. His philosophy was practical to achieving world peace and at no expense to anyone. It was built on simple common sense, but sometimes common sense defies logic.

He continued, "America is not the land of milk and honey as the world truly believes. On the contrary, but it has a stable government unlike most oil-rich countries in the Middle East. Democracy and stability can bring peace and prosperity. On the other hand, dictators milk their country's wealth dry then export their heist to other friendly countries. When leaders become fathers or mothers and treat their citizens with honesty and respect, then their countries will be a heavenly place. Desperate journeys by their citizens will be an event of the past. Papa, the root of all evil is money. Is it true that the purpose of money and wealth is to help others? Why then is it that the rich get richer and the poor get poorer? Every government gives tax breaks to the wealthy at the expense of the hardworking middle class.

I will give a few examples of abuse of power and money. These leaders were not filthy rich. They were stinking rich at the expense of the poor masses of their countries. Gaddafi in Libya was worth over two hundred billion. This corrupt dictator had real estate, bank accounts, and corporate investments all around the world. However, majority of his people were starving. His people rebelled against his tyranny. He went from living in celestial palaces to hiding like a rodent in a filthy canal, struggling for his last breath of life. His people dragged him through the streets then shot him to death in Sirte. The proud dictator begged like a crying baby for his people to spare his life. Sadly, he never enjoyed his vast stolen wealth. He could have given every citizen a million dollars and remain with one hundred and fifty billion.

President Hosni Mubarak of Egypt was worth over seven hundred billion. He was charged for political corruption and embezzling state funds. In 2012, the Egyptian court sentenced Mubarak to prison. He died in prison. Poor guy never enjoyed his billions. Nearer at home, Dictator Fidel Castro, according to *Forbes* magazine, has accumulated wealth to at least nine hundred million dollars. The Cuban dictator runs Cuba as if it were his own farm and eleven million poor starving Cubans as his slaves. Every day, thousands of starving Cubans try desperately to escape from Cuba by any means possible. Fidel Castro died never enjoying his wealth. The Cuban people are still living in prison under his brother, Rahul Castro. Has the removal of trade embargo helped the Cuban people? No, no, the head of the snake is still the vicious Castro. Ali Abdullah Saleh of Yemen was worth over sixty billion dollars. For years, the Americans saw Ali as a very important political ally in their fight against Al-Qaeda and terrorism. His people were starving. Forty percent of Yemen's population earned less than two dollars per day. Civil wars have ruined that once prosperous country.

It is no wonder then that The Holy Bible clearly proclaims that it is easier for a camel to pass through the eye of a needle than for a rich man to get to heaven. Strangely enough, Evangelist pastors here in the USA continue to swindle their flocks with open eyes their hard-earned dollars in the name of the high God. They live in palaces suitable for kings. They have their own private planes yet they preach to their followers about humility and sharing. If there is truly a hell, then there a special place for these money-hungry bastards."

After those venomous words, Krishna sat motionless and took a deep breath. His eyes were closed as he relaxed under the cool breeze of the full moon night. His audience was totally engrossed in his discourse. He continued deep in thought, "What I said previously is extremely relevant to what I am going to say now. Lord Jesus said in the Bible that faith without works is dead. It means that in this life, you must be honest and help others in your quest to enter the gates of heaven. Therefore, man—in some form—is rewarded equally for his charitable deeds or his unwarranted hostile actions. Every religious culture speaks about accountability for your actions as good or bad, yin-yang, or karma."

Krishna smiled as he slowly sipped his tea. "Science and religion do seek to better our lives. I want to touch briefly about the science of reincarnation. Eastern philosophy teaches that when the physical body dies, the soul is reborn into another body. I will give some startling, factual, yet amazing accounts. In Delhi, India, 1930, four-year-old Shanti Devi tells her family that in her previous life, she was a woman named Lugdi Bai and that she had lived in a nearby village of Mathura. At first, the parents thought she was crazy, and they wanted to dismiss her story as a childhood fantasy. The child persisted because she knew so much about her other fantasy world. She pestered her parents until they decided to investigate her claims. They traveled to the place in question. While there, she went to meet her previous husband and his new wife. He also, after talking to her, believed that the child was the reincarnation of his previous wife. Lugdi Bai, his previous wife, had died in childbirth. Mahatma Gandhi got involved in this fantastic story and launched a in-depth investigation. Gandhi was satisfied that she was a reincarnation of Lugdi Bai. Hindus strongly believe that when the person dies, the soul is reborn in a new body.

This physical body is simply a vessel for the soul. Death is a spiritual resurrection of the soul."

Krishna raised his teacup in Ahmed's direction. He smiled and continued, "Brother-in-law, you are right. True science does not contradict God's teachings. The History Channel showed a remarkable documentary about reincarnation. When they examine evidence, a consistent theme emerges—what they found in multiple cases of people who have bizarre birthmarks who then accurately remembered having been someone else in the past life. In some these instances, they can confirm that in their past life, a person died in a certain way, and they come back with a corresponding bizarre mark in the same area. For example, if they died by gunshot, we know where the gunshot wound took place. The person reincarnates, and they have a birthmark right where the gunshot entered. Is it possible then that a birthmark could be the consciousness creating a physical manifestation that happened in a life?"

Krishna paused for a moment to look at everyone. Ahmed remarked cleverly, "Continue, my brother, with your many theories."

Krishna smiled confidently, "Reincarnation is not a theory but a science. My discourse does not seek to the convert anyone but to enlighten everyone with an open mind."

My silence on such profound philosophy showed my utter ignorance on this educational and fascinating subject. Am I the only ignorant one on this important subject? Was it a story, myth, or fact? Levelheaded Krishna seemed convinced that reincarnation was factual and relevant to Western culture. My son continued, "Does our soul die with our physical body? Its mysterious nature continues to fascinate different areas of science. Now a group of researchers has discovered a new truth about it—that the soul does not die. It returns to the universe.

"Since 1996, Dr. Stuart Hameroff, an American physicist and emeritus in the department of anesthesiology and psychology, and Sir Roger Penrose, a mathematical physicist at Oxford University, worked in a quantum theory of consciousness in which they stated that the soul is maintained in microtubules of the brain cells. Dr. Hameroff said, 'Let's say the heart stops flowing. The microtubules lose their quantum state. The quantum information within the microtubules is not destroyed. It cannot be destroyed, and it just distributes and dissipates to the universe at large. If the patient is a resuscitated, revived, this quantum information can go back into the microtubules, and the patient can say that they had a near-death experience. If they are not revived and the patient dies, it is possible that this quantum information can exist outside the body, perhaps indefinitely, as a soul.'"

Ahmed laughed. He retorted, "Your philosophy is surely like a fairy tale not a man of science. Those teachings are irrelevant to my way of life."

Nevertheless, Krishna continued unperturbed by Ahmed's sarcastic remarks. Maria added, "This information is totally new to me. I was raised in a Catholic home. We only read the Bible."

Krishna added, "Good, but we must read all scriptures regardless of our beliefs. Working with refugees worldwide, I became involved in people's diverse cultures and varying religious beliefs. I have realized that none is superior or inferior to the other. Another question arises. Are we alone on this universe? Every day, astronomers are discovering new planets. Yes, my friends, we are not alone in this vast universe. In 1971, NASA astronaut Edgar Mitchell became the sixth person to walk on the moon. He once claimed that peace-loving aliens had visited Earth on a mission to save humanity from nuclear war and suggested the Vatican knows the truth about the existence of extraterrestrials. Mitchell also alleged that UFOs had been seen above nuke bases and often disabled the missiles held within Cold War era weapons silos."

I added, "Son, what you are saying sounds like a science fiction movie."

Krishna laughed heartily. He held my hand gently. "Papa, the History Channel had a series on time travel. They quote an account from the Mahabharata. In this sacred Indian text written in eighth century BC, King Revaita is described as traveling to the heavens to meet with the Creator.

"This Hindu version may be the oldest record of successful time travel in the ancient past. King Revaita was taken into space to see the gods. When he returns to earth, he finds that many ages have gone by, and it's been hundreds of years. This is the kind of thing that would happen to space travelers. You think that you are gone for only a few days, but when you return to earth, you find out that you have been gone hundreds of years. Are these incidents fairy tales or scientific facts? The Hindu epic text Mahabharata is loaded with apparent examples from flying vehicles to voice-activated weapons and even events that sound like nuclear detonations. Lord Shiva has a third eye that when opened, destroys all that is seen. Ancient alien theorists point out that Shiva is often shown surrounded by a circle of flames. Could this be him inside a fiery craft? It is like many other chariot myths with the likes of Oden and Zeus.

"In closing my long and boring conversation, death is not a great calamity but a natural process in the existence of a being as a separate entity, a resting period during which it recuperates, reassembles its resources, adjusts its course, and returns again to the earth to continue its journey. Are they myths, a fantasy of my wild imagination or facts? Like a seed buried in the sand, it dies then springs to life. Our death is like that seed waiting to spring to life. In the Bible, the book of Job 14:1–2,14 states that man born of woman is of few days and full of trouble springs up like a flower and withers away, like a fleeting shadow, he does not endure... If a man dies, he will live again. The Bible tells us that there is not only life after death but eternal life so glorious that no one has seen nor ear has heard, and no mind has imagined what God has prepared for those that love him. You are the master of your destiny on this journey called life."

Krishna placed his hands on my shoulders. He looked at me straight into my eyes with reassurance. "Papa, one day, we will be reunited with your sons and my brothers, Tom and John, in more euphoric surroundings. I think we had a long boring night."

Everyone laughed. Thunder and lightning filled the night sky. It started to rain heavily. Ahmed departed with a Uber taxi. Without thinking, I bade farewell to everyone and rushed to my car in the pouring rain. To my surprise, my car was nowhere in sight. Then it struck me that I had parked illegally there. I was soaking wet. My son realized my dilemma. He insisted that I spend the night at his home. He said, "Papa, please overnight at my home. Maria is overnighting in my guest bedroom. She leaves for Orlando early in the morning. Tomorrow, we will go and pay the fine and retrieve your car. Call Mama and tell her of your plans. We can share my bed."

Krishna saw the nervousness in my eyes when I mentioned Dr. Maria. He teasingly reassured me, "Papa, I know women. Maria will be spending the night here before traveling to Orlando. Is it safe for a woman alone to be driving a long distance in this horrible weather? Do you think so? We are close friends, not intimate friends. We are not friends with benefits. I know what is on your analytical mind."

I added, "Son, honestly I was just thinking of your safety."

We both laughed at my awkward line of questioning. My heart was now at ease. Frankly, after my encounter with Jose, I did not want my son to encounter a similar fate. There is a saying that a snake is a snake. The creature will shed its skin, but it is the same snake.

CHAPTER SIX

A Journey Into
Incurable Diseases

Marriage, family relationship and friendship become tested when incurable diseases encroach in our lives like a thief in the night or an unwanted wart in an uncomfortable place. They become an entangled web and an integral part and parcel of the unwanted equation in our lives. The real test of metal of a strong relationship is caring and loving your partner even when there is a disappearing glimmer of bleakness. Loving and living have no warranty. A marriage contract is not worth the value of the paper that is written on if both parties fight like cats and dogs or the famous cartoon such as *Tom and Jerry*.

In marriage, there is a dependence on each other for love and caring, especially when illness become part of the equation. In a harmonious relationship, there is no independence. True love is depending on each other for comfort, love, and support in sickness and health. The human body is a fragile one, susceptible to numerous deadly diseases. Does it matter how much nutritious foods that you consume daily or how much you work out? Is our destiny written in the stars regardless of our positive habits? Is the phrase, 'We are what we eat' true? Maybe it is what eats us deep inside our subconscious. Does a fiery temper make our body more susceptible to incurable diseases? Sri Sathya Sai Baba said, "When the mind is sick, the body becomes sick."

Doctors now believe that there must be complete harmony of the mind, body, and spirit to be healthy. When incurable diseases become part of our lives, divorce and unfaithfulness enter. This chapter touches on the very soul of every human being because suffering and diseases touch every fabric of our daily lives. Incurable diseases tear families apart or bring the family unit closer together.

This chapter will surely bring tears to your eyes. To every human being, these desperate journeys are real and true. Sadly, as I am writing this book, thousands of suffering patients are succumbing to incurable ailments, such as cancer, HIV, ALS, multiple sclerosis, and many, many more. Is it more profitable for the pharmaceutical companies to treat symptoms rather than researching a cure? A practical solution for every country is cutting their expenditure on weapons of mass destruction instead allocating more funds to save lives and the Planet Earth. Why are there no cures for common diseases, such as tooth cavities or diabetes, which existed for centuries?

There will be no need for the trillion of dollars spent on artificial sweeteners, sodas, or low-calorie desserts every year. Cure means no profits. Lou Gehrig's disease, or ALS, is an autoimmune disease. Every year, organizations collect billions of dollars through fund-raising, yet how much of that money actually goes into research to find a cure? How much money goes toward helping ALS patients in their everyday lives? By nature, or the laws of natural selection, the human body is prone to many incurable diseases. Our human body does not come with a warranty for good health.

I hugged Krishna and bade farewell. "Tell Maria," I said, "Drive safely. I passed by her room, and she was snoring loudly. Son, please stay away from her like you should avoid the plague. Anyway, it is better that I go to the police impound alone to retrieve my car with Uber. After all, you have a houseguest. Stay away from Maria. She is trouble."

When I mentioned snoring, my son laughed loudly. Did I snore heavily? My wife, Anita nags me relentlessly about my irritating snoring. She said that I am a carpenter at bedtime and a headshrinker in the day. When, I inquired why, she said that my irritating snoring is like a carpenter sawing wood every night.

As I departed from my son's home, he said confidently, "Papa, I am a big boy now. I know the crafty ways of the female species."

Twenty minutes later, my Nigerian Uber driver reached the police impound. For the full length of my ride, he moaned nonstop of the difficulties of living in Florida. He said respectfully that in America, there was no equality of races.

In the police impound, I was rudely lectured by a fat, potbelly police officer. He trounced on me like a hungry bear with a severe tongue-lashing. He barked loudly to an unwelcomed and embarrassed audience at the impound office. I was pleasantly amused at his crazy antics.

He stuttered, "You… you rich… rich people believe that because you… you have money, it gives you… you the right to park anywhere. You were parked in the darkness of the night in a 'no parking' zone around a blind corner. There were no streetlights. Your selfish action could have caused someone to get killed last night."

He was right. My apology was sincere and from the heart. "I am really, really sorry, officer. You are right. My actions were wrong. Again, I am sorry."

He barked louder again, "I do not want to see your ugly face here again!"

My mind was thrown in confusion, and then it dawned upon me. This officer needs to see a good Psychiatrist. Did he know that I am a Psychiatrist? Was he playing mind games with me? Was he suffering from posttraumatic stress disorder, or was he just a plain bully?

I just smiled and ignored his taunts. Life is too short to get irritated about everything. A smile is priceless. As I drove to our restaurant, my mind was in a state of euphoria. Krishna's tranquil words resonated in my ears with his unusual concept of life. His words were honest and from the heart. 'Papa, one day, you will be reunited with Tom and John under more pleasant and joyous circumstances. There will be an everlasting peace in your lives someday.'

Every Sunday morning at our restaurant, my wife Anita arranged to have a series of guest speakers for brunch. Today our guest speaker was born in Trinidad; therefore, they are serving that island's foods. I started to drive faster to reach on time. I smiled and waved at every stranger driving alongside me, knowing that there was certainly life after death. My medical training was devoid of such theories, fairy tales, and fantasies. At our restaurant, I was greeted with so much hugs and kisses. It is true that absence makes the heart grow fonder. Lisa, my daughter hugged me like there were no tomorrow. She looked at me lovingly and said, "Daddy, we must hurry inside. You are very late as usual. Pharmacist and author Saisnath Baijoo is giving a brief lecture, followed by his book signing on incurable diseases."

She grabbed my hands and literally dragged me to our auditorium like a ragged doll. We reached the hall in a few minutes. It was packed to capacity. Foods were plentiful on every table. My mouth started to dribble from hunger as I crave for some spicy Trini foods.

My daughter is strong and robust. She is six feet tall. She can easily beat any man in physical combat. She has a red belt in martial arts. We finally reached our reserved seats in the front of the auditorium. I nagged Lisa that I was famished, but she totally ignored my hunger plead. She waved to the author. He motioned us to come to the podium quickly. Lisa promptly dragged me again. At the podium, the author stood to greet us politely. This robust, muscular man had a pleasant euphoric smile. His grip was strong as he shook my frail hand. After our polite salutations, Lisa dragged me again to our seats. Noticeably absent from our table was my wife, Anita. I looked around the enormous auditorium; she was nowhere to be found here. At our table, Ahmed, Lisa's husband, and my handsome chubby grandson ate ravenously. My daughter motioned our waiter to bring our preordered meal. The lecture was about to begin. Saisnath Baijoo, our guest speaker, rose to give his discourse.

He waved his hand robustly, then pounded his chest, finally clasped his hands together, and bowed reverently. Baijoo gently tapped on the microphone gently a few times and said, "Can anyone hear me clearly in the back of the room? Please wave and smile if you can hear me."

From the back of the room, everyone waved in acknowledgment. He sat for a few moments and played nervously with his glasses and his folder. He rose quickly from his chair. His spirited voice resonated across the large auditorium. "Thank you for spending your precious time with me on this beautiful, sunny Florida morning. Anyone in this audience that is not stricken with an incurable disease or their loved ones cannot and will not fully appreciate the depth and trauma that is involuntarily dispensed to an unfortunate one."

With these authoritative words, the audience automatically stopped eating. Were they shell-shocked? The audience was hungry to hear more from their guest speaker. The seasoned speaker had everyone's undivided attention. He continued, "Their death sentence has already served. It is only a matter of time before their demise. To these unfortunate ones, their deathbed becomes their solace, strength, and a comforting refuge. Many secret tears are shed in solitude.

Unless you walk in their shoes, you cannot understand the depth of pain, suffering, and trauma. In solace, they ask the eternal questions. 'Why me, God? What did I ever do to deserve this suffering? I have always lived a good live. I never hurt anyone. Why me, Lord?' These incurable diseases have severed families. Divorces are rampant. Unfaithfulness may become part and parcel of this new relationship. The true mettle of 'until death do us part' has been tried and tested to its utmost core. It is truly comforting to hug a dying loved one and say, 'Everything is all right. I am with you always.' Is it false hope or comfort? In a devoted marriage, there is love, respect, trust, understanding, friendship, and faith that is a necessary recipe for incurable diseases. When your partner suffers, you feel their pain. In some cases, the partner moans, 'How will I survive?' rather than 'How can I help my suffering and dying loved one?'

Self becomes more important rather than the welfare of the tormented ones. Loved ones not only need your prayers but your unconditional support physically, mentally, spiritually, and financially. Love is sharing their last dreams. It is giving the afflicted one a fountain of love. It is listening with empathy. It is about drying their many tears, squelching their fears, and cheering for their every miniscule success. A warm smile, a comforting hug, and a tender heart help your ailing patient to survive longer and with the genuine reassurance that they are surrounded with security and love. Their road to survival is paved with numerous obstacles and blind corners. Do not be that obstacle, but be a comforter, a tower of strength, a lighthouse of hope, and a friend every day all the way."

The author paused for a brief moment. His back was turned away from the audience. His speech was truly from the heart. I looked at the audience from my vantage point. Everyone was extremely quiet and focused on his every movements. You could hear a pin drop. He turned to the audience with a tranquil smile.

"My friends, my name is Saisnath Baijoo. I am a pharmacist and author here in Miami. My birthplace is Trinidad in the West Indies. I am a victim of Lou Gehrig's disease, or amyotrophic lateral sclerosis, or ALS. According to my many learned doctors, it is an incurable disease. Nevertheless, God puts his toughest soldiers to fight the roughest battles. In the frontline, I am one of those soldiers fighting a battle for survival. No matter what the world throws at me, I smile whether it is good or bad. In the Bible, in the book of Job, he was a God-fearing and prosperous man. God intentionally removed Job's wealth, his children, and his physical health from his life. Despite all his difficult circumstances, he never cursed God. Job said that his miserable earthly condition was simply God's will. Is our sickness dictated by some higher power or our own bad eating habits?

From my experience in Miami, 99 percent of doctors know nothing about this ALS disease. You see, doctors are proudly called practicing physicians. They are still practicing to get it right. You are presumed dead in two years after an ALS diagnosis. My learned doctors do know for certain that the disease is progressive. What do they really mean by progressive? It means that the disease will kill you sooner than later. I told my practicing neurologist jokingly who had no sense of humor, 'Our life is progressive. When we live one day, we are dead to that day. When we celebrate our thirty-fifth birthday, we have progressively died for thirty-five years.' He looked at me like he wanted to prescribe antidepressants. I guess he did not like my silly statements. I have a dream that someday a cure will be discovered for motor neuron diseases."

The audience stood on their feet and applauded for a few minutes. They were hungry for more of his heartwarming yet emotional speech. The speaker waved his hands and motioned his audience to take their seats. I was famished, but his speech was more interesting. He wanted to continue his discourse.

"I am divorced not by my choice. I do not know if I have ever experienced the real meaning of true love. Have you? True love has always been elusive in my life. Make no mistake. Love is an honorable word to those who are honest and sincere. Do not be angry of partners or people who forsake you. They have lost many treasures. Marriage is like a deck of cards. In the beginning, all that you need are two hearts and some diamonds. When things turn sour, you wish you held a club and some spades. Remember, diamond is a girl's best friend, but a dog is a man's best friend."

Laughter filled the large auditorium. The audience rose to their feet and clapped thunderously. Baijoo motioned the audience to be seated again.

"You see, my friends in life, people were created to be loved and care for others. Things or material wealth were created to be used to improve our lives. The world has turned upside down. Things are loved and cherished like your iPhone, and people have been used to further other people's ambitions. 'My life sucks' is not in my vocabulary. I cannot recreate or change my past, but I can surely build a concrete foundation for the present and future. Incurable disease makes your future hazy like there is no tomorrow. Is there a tomorrow? Sadly, no. When tomorrow comes, it is today. *Impossible* means 'hopeless,' but the same word can be broken into 'I'm possible.' God is called by many names, but to everyone who trusts him with a pure heart, then everything is possible. Make the impossible, possible.

ALS cripples your muscles, making walking difficult. Every footstep is a challenge and a conquest. ALS impedes your speech. You have no sense of balance. Using a walker is a necessity for me. ALS victims needs your encouragement not your pity.

"I quote from a fellow ALS victim. Her name is Nancy.

I am venting my feelings on Facebook. My husband has abandoned me for a younger woman. My children want to put me in a twenty-four-hour day care. Family members do not care again for me. They have disowned me. All my so-called friends have denied my existence on this earth. I am truly alone. Facebook friends are superficial. I am tired of crying. Money and sickness show the true colors of family and friends. This world has forsaken me. I am truly alone. Everyone has abandoned me. Why?

My friends, reach out and touch someone. Be a friend."

Everyone was quiet. You could hear a pin drop on the floor. Our speaker was struggling to keep his balance on the podium. He sat and continued with his discourse.

"Leaving a strong and everlasting legacy is everyone's dream, something for a loved one to remember when you are gone. Your life is defined by how we deal with our problems. This poem says it all.

Dying Young
Eileen Manassian

> I'm afraid of dying young
> Of leaving things yet undone
> I'm afraid I'll leave this place
> Yet not leave a single trace
> I'm afraid I haven't said
> All that lives inside my head
> I'm afraid I'll disappear
> And no one will hold me dear.

"My friends, leave a legacy of love for a dying one. Leave a smile on their face, not a frown. Unwanted frustration and worries only accelerate their demise. According to science, true love prolongs life. Nevertheless, I remain positive that soon a treatment or a cure will be discovered for ALS. My fellow sufferers, never give up. Never give up hope, even when the world has forsaken you. Thank you for your time and support. It was certainly a pleasure being here. Remember, God never promised you an easy life but an easy landing. Life's journey is unpredictable and heartbreaking, but there are moments of happiness. In your darkest hours, look for a silver lining in every dark cloud.

Never abuse or misuse people who care for you. Always remember the ones that cared for you. Thank you."

Everyone stood on their feet to clap continuously for an emotional speech. Lisa leaned on my shoulder with tears in her eyes.

"Daddy, this guy is really a dynamic and energetic speaker despite his ALS illness. Please invite him to our table for lunch. Please, Daddy." Lisa hugged me tightly. I could not refuse such a loving request. The audience was still on their feet as author Baijoo bowed in acknowledgment of his heartbreaking and emotional speech.

Finally, my beautiful wife, Anita walked unto the podium gracefully and embraced the speaker. She walked with poise to the microphone to speak. "On behalf of my enthusiastic audience, I want to thank you, my friend, for that intense speech. Never give up regardless of the odds stacked against you. You are a walking legend and a living inspiration to us all."

The audience rose to their feet to give another thunderous applause. The author acknowledged their applause by bowing and clasping his hands again. Tears poured from his wary eyes, but he had a fragrant yet tranquil smile. This was truly a very touching occasion, a moment in time that I will not forget easily. I was truly touched by his passionate speech, a dialogue straight from his bleeding heart. The world had forsaken him except for his immediate family, yet he was such a positive and dynamic speaker. I love his positive attitude toward life.

Anita escorted the speaker toward our table. She rushed to give me a kiss on my lips. She turned toward her guest and proudly announced, "This is my family—my husband Jonathan, my daughter Lisa, and her husband, Ahmed. This is the love of my life, Akram, my grandson. My son, Krishna will be here shortly." Anita bowed her head for minute then continued, "My two other sons died a few months ago."

Realizing the distress in Anita's words, I intervened in their conversation. "Mr. Baijoo, sir, it is certainly a pleasure to meet you. Can we continue this conversation over lunch? I am starving. I could eat horses."

Baijoo paused for a moment then added, "Just call me Baijoo, my friend."

He turned away from me and gently held my wife's hand. He looked at her with grave apprehension. "I am truly sorry for your tragic loss. It is not easy losing loved ones. Be brave. God is watching over you. Have confidence and rest assured that one day, you will be reunited with your loved ones. Death is merely a transition to another life. What is most important is that you have the support of a lovely family. Be brave and never give up. My friend, Jonathan, I cannot eat a horse, but some good nutritious food will be deeply appreciated."

My wife led us to a private dining area. Our guest followed closely with his walker. His gait was uneven and unsteady. He was struggling to walk even with the assistance of his walker, yet he never complained about anything. We sat to have a scrumptious meal. Dr. Maria and Krishna joined our table.

Krishna introduced Maria to everyone as a close friend. I concluded that my son Krishna was having an affair with Maria. My mind, for a moment, was troubled, thinking about Maria and Krishna. The night before, I had warned my son about Maria with these tough words: "Maria is an evil snake. A snake changes its skin, but it is the same snake. Maria will not be a faithful wife or girlfriend. She is a player. Son, you are playing with fire. You will get burned severely."

Krishna read my mind as I steered in his direction. He sat on the chair next to me. He quickly wrote on a napkin to me, "Two single and lonely people looking for a one-night stand."

My heart was gripped with fear. He jokingly wrote on another napkin, "Ha, ha, old man, nothing happened. No drama. Maria's vehicle had a flat tire. We called AAA. They took their casual time to come to my home. After brunch, she is driving to Orlando."

My conspiracy theory on Maria were put to rest at least for the present time. Meanwhile, our guest speaker picked his food. My attention was now focused on him. Baijoo was more interested in having a conversation rather than his scrumptious meal. Was he a lonely man? To be the victim of ALS and divorce at the same time is truly distressing. My patients firmly believe that their world has come to an end after their divorce. They beg for anxiety medications, antidepressants, and sleeping tablets.

Here is a man who was decreed a divorce in addition to fighting an incurable disease. Nevertheless, he seemed at peace with the world. His laughter was euphoric yet contagious. He did not want sympathy or pity. Baijoo wanted to have a discussion rather than eat a scrumptious meal. He turned his attention to a journey of different nature.

His voice became more mellowed as he told of a heart-wrenching account of his loving sister's desperate battle with the deadly breast cancer. He grieved, "Medals are given for outstanding achievements. Medals are not given for those who have positively transformed the lives of those around them. Medals will fade away, but memories are embedded in our subconscious forever. The neighbors called affectionately my sister simply Mama. She was loved by everyone. Mama's home was a warm, welcoming one. There was always a meal for everyone at any time and any day. Mama was a devoted Hindu, yet she participated in diverse kinds of religious functions. She believed that it was not their religious affiliation but rather their loving commitment and sincerity toward God and people that was important in life. Her devotion and love to God and family were unmatched by no one.

Our parents worked in the sugarcane estates under slavery conditions. Despite having two small children, she felt that it was her moral obligation to help her parents in the sugarcane fields. We spent quality time fishing in the Caroni River, an activity she enjoyed immensely. Mama was a devoted nanny to my children. She loved and adored them like her own children.

After noticing a lump on her breast, her doctor diagnosed cancer. Mama followed her doctor's advice to the letter. She was a strong soul and a fighter. When I migrated to Miami, she came to visit me. Our bond as brother and sister grew even stronger. She wanted to visit Disney World. I gladly obliged. At the happiest place on earth, she was totally exhausted after a short while. She refused to move one inch or centimeter. From my observation, she was losing weight rapidly, yet she joked, 'My brother, my sexy body is no more. Only my frame and bones are here.' I held her hand to comfort her. She cried. We said nothing. On our return journey to Miami, she slept like a baby. However, she jokingly said to me, 'Little brother, if you are going fishing, please wake me up. I am really dog-tired but not for fishing.' Little moments like fishing thrilled her with passion. Everyone was laughing at her desire to go fishing. One hour later, on reaching Fort Pierce, I stopped to find an ideal area to fish for cascadura and tilapias. Mama was very excited despite the lurking presence of alligators and crocodiles in the lake. Her frail body had received a boost of inner strength at the word *fishing*. She was ecstatic. I knew that she was in severe pain, yet she never complained to no one. As the fishing net was pulled near her, Mama was overjoyed to see the large fishes that we caught in my net."

Baijoo looked delighted to see the joy on his ailing sister's face.

"Mama rejoiced and shouted that we will have a party tonight. On reaching my home in Miami, Mama volunteered for the demanding task of cleaning the fishes. Her tranquil mood was enhanced by the chirping of the birds in my rose garden. She smiled and looked at me with solid assurance. She held my hand. 'My dear brother, my journey on this earth is coming to an end... Do not shed tears for me. My God knows what is best for my life. One day, we will meet again.' We hugged each other and cried. Then, she said with that ever confident and euphoric smile, 'I have made peace with my God. He is ready to receive me into his kingdom. Brother, I am not afraid of dying. Please remember me. We had fond memories together. I have truly loved your children like my own kids. I love you.' After leaving Miami, I spent two weeks at her home in Trinidad. During that time, all our family took Mama to Maracas Beach. She was full of joy. A few months later, she died peacefully at her home."

Baijoo paused for a moment. Tears filled his eyes. Everyone was silent. Lisa reached out and touched his frail hands. She added softly, "I am so sorry for your loss."

Baijoo smiled. "Humans cannot comprehend death but it is are inevitable. It is a merely a journey and a transition to another life."

Lisa continued, "Krishna and I worked in West Africa during the deadly Ebola outbreak. Death stared us every day. Aid workers believe that the residents did not trust their medical help with their ailing love ones. They hid them in their homes. They never went to the hospital when they contracted hemorrhagic fever or explosive diarrhea. They stayed at home and unknowingly infecting everyone in their household. Sadly, a few health-care workers died while trying to help fight Ebola. HIV and Ebola are decimating the economic growth of those affected countries. Africa is home to about 15.2 percent of the world population. Thirty-five million are HIV-infected and fifteen million have died already. Sad, but it is a reality of life."

Dr. Maria laughed. "Men are like animals. They want too much sexual partners. They want to treat women like in the movie, *Fifty Shades of Grey.* I am no man's slave."

I looked at my son Krishna and smiled. I jokingly responded with a pointed question, "I see, but only men are cheaters?"

Lisa looked at me, very visibly amused at my sly comment, but continued, "With regards to the HIV virus, here in the United States of America, we are not far behind. In this country, there are more than a million people who have tested positive for HIV virus. Sadly, one in seven doesn't know if they have contracted this incurable disease."

Maria was silent and obviously uncomfortable with the trend of our present conversation. She abruptly rose from her seat and remarked, "Guys, thank you for your kind invitation, but I must be on my way. I would like to reach Orlando before it gets dark. Krishna, my love, please call me anytime."

Krishna responded with a smile, "Sorry, my love, but I need to focus on my family. We have been through some troubling times."

Maria's facial expression changed from a seductive smile to a sarcastic and venomous tone directed at my son. "My love, married couples find time to raise their children and have prosperous careers. Nevertheless, they still find time to cheat on their unsuspecting partners. My darling, you are single and still have no time for a sexy and educated woman like me." With those cynical words, Maria hastily departed from our restaurant.

Fast forward, two months later, Maria and her American lover were found dead in his sprawling ranch in Homestead. They had apparently committed suicide with the use of two deadly cyanide injections. There was a deceptive note written on their bed: "Perfect people don't drink, don't lie, don't cheat, don't fight, don't complain, and don't exist. Goodbye world.'

The investigating officers were not totally convinced that it was a double suicide. They were mystified. Their inquiry would be an ongoing one. When I heard of the tragic news on my television, I was not surprised at the outcome of Dr. Maria's life. My response was simple: "Sad, sad. A waste of talent. Karma is a bitch. When you live by the sword, then someday you may fall on your sword."

CHAPTER SEVEN

A Journey Not by Choice

Back to the present time at our restaurant's Sunday brunch, at our dining table, I asked Baijoo simply, "My friend, does Lou Gehrig's disease gives you any muscular pain? I am also a victim of this dreadful disease. Dr. Ahmed, my son-in-law, performed a stem cell procedure. The results are debatable."

Baijoo contemplated for a moment and answered, "Firstly, for ALS victims, every footstep is a challenge and a victory. Falls may result in concussion and could be fatal. ALS associations have periodic collection drive, but how much of that money goes toward caring about ALS patients in their everyday living? Ah, my friends, no one cares. This is a dog eat world or a rat race. Secondly, with regards to Maria's statement about being no man's slave, that reminds me of the movie, *Fifty Shades of Gray*. Honestly, I am divorced three times. I am no woman's slave," Baijoo joked. He continued, "Everyone is a slave at some time to someone in their lives. Therefore, my old heart is immune to pain. Parents slave and sacrifice to ensure that their children get the right education. Is that slavery? No, my friends, it is a moral obligation."

We all laughed at Baijoo's agile ability to play with words. Since brunch time, no one had left our dining table. It was now time for lunchtime. Our bellies were grumbling for more food. Still sitting at our table were Lisa, Krishna, Anita, Baijoo, Ahmed, and the author of this book, yours truly, Jonathan. My poor heart skipped a beat as I shouted without thinking, "Where is my handsome grandson, Akram?"

Lisa laughed and gently added, "Relax, Grandpa. He is with Nana Joe in the play area."

I lowered my voice. "You know kidnapping of children is very common."

The renowned author added, "Dr. Maria briefly mentioned slavery. That is a dreadful word. Have you ever wondered whether invading countries like England, Spain, France, and Holland teach their schoolchildren the plain truth about their past slaughters and genocide of friendly natives in their conquered lands? History books seem devoid of the truth of the atrocious acts committed by these savage conquerors. For example, Christopher Columbus is bestowed with a holiday here in the United States of America for his great heroic conquest. However, this blundering hero never reached the shores of the mainland United States. His goal was really finding a sea route to India. He went the wrong way. With their European diseases, like chicken pox, and guns, they decimated millions of natives in a brief time. Their heinous crimes were sugarcoated to protect their conscience and the blessed images of their countries. The English and Spanish portrayed themselves as saviors of these savages and uncivilized races. Their goals were saving the souls of these heathens from eternal damnation in the name of Christianity. However, the Inca Empire was the largest pre-Columbian empire in the Americas and, possibly, the largest in the world in the sixteenth century. They had instituted a system of government superior to any European power. They developed a calendar year of 365 days.

Nevertheless, in the beginning, these heathens welcomed the Europeans with open arms. Let me stress clearly that the conquerors were only interested in the vast untapped material wealth of their newly conquered lands. On the other side of the globe, India at first welcomed the British as mutual trading partners willing to purchase their vast array of exports. At that time, India was booming in trade and technology. In medicine, Indians were performing plastic surgery as early as sixth century BC. Sushruta, one of the earliest recorded surgeons, vividly describes the basic principles of plastic surgery in his famous ancient treatise, Sushruta Samhita. Compared to the Europeans, Indians were very highly advanced in mathematics, science, astronomy, architecture, government, and writing. Their ancient books—like the Vedas, Upanishads, Bhagavad Gita, Ramayana—are still relevant today. Education was given prominence in ancient India since early Vedic civilization. Nalanda University in Bihar was established in the early fifth century. By the way, my forefathers came from Bihar as indentured servants, another fancy name for slaves.

From earliest times, students from countries like Korea, Japan, China, Tibet, Indonesia, Persia, and Turkey traveled to Bihar, India, for education. Here, they studied grammar, philosophy, Ayurveda medicine, agriculture, surgery, politics, agriculture, astronomy, commerce, and religion. In 2010, the Parliament in India approved a plan to restore ancient Nalanda University as a modern Nalanda International University dedicated for postgraduate research. Asian countries like China, Singapore, and Japan gladly assisted in the funding. When the African slaves were freed, the Indians were contracted to work as Indentured laborers in the sugar estates throughout the vast British Empire.

Before the time of Christ, the Roman Empire was buying vast quantities of textiles and spices from India.

When the British invaded India, they very amazed at the magnificent architecture like the Taj Mahal. When the British were forced to leave in India in 1947, they left India broken and penniless. Thereafter, famine followed, causing millions to die. In granting India independence, the British separated India along religious lines—a Muslim India called Pakistan and a Hindu India called Bharat or India. Gandhi objected vehemently in vain to this religious separation. This partition caused millions to die in cross border migrations. The British knew that utter chaos would follow their callous actions. They stood and watched delightedly as their planned disaster unfolded according to their heartless actions. Their soldiers did nothing to stop the mayhem."

Lisa interrupted, "My brother, Krishna and I have traveled extensively throughout Africa and India. I truly agree that the greatest crimes in the history of the world committed by conquering nations is that of slavery. Millions of enslaved people made a desperate journey without their choice completely separated from their families. Human cargoes were transported thousands of miles by perilous sea into foreign lands. During that death-defying journey, they were shackled in chains throughout the months at sea. Even in chains, the captors were beaten, starved, and tortured into submission. Their names, cultures, and languages were substituted for that of their conquerors. Here is a quotation from an English press. Having conquered vast territory, the British authorities sat in their golden thrones and decided how to make their conquest more profitable. Lord Macaulay, addressing the British Parliament on February 2, 1835, said,

> I have travelled across the length and breadth of India and I have not seen one person who is a beggar, who is a thief such wealth I have seen in this country, such high moral values, people of such caliber, that I do not think we would ever conquer this country, unless we break the very backbone of this nation, which is her spiritual and cultural heritage and therefore, I propose that we replace her old and ancient education system, her culture, for if the Indians think that all that is foreign and English is good and greater than their own, they will lose their self-esteem, their native culture and they will become what we want them, a truly dominated nation.

"Sad but true. The conqueror dictates the fate of these unfortunate souls. They decreed a new language, culture, new government, and new names for their unwilling subjects."

Anita interrupted her daughter, "My love, the Bible mentions slavery on numerous occasions. It does not condemn this practice. In fact, Ephesians 6:5 says that 'Slaves, obey your earthly masters with deep respect and fear. Serve them sincerely as you would serve Christ.'"

Krishna added, "Arab slave trade was active throughout the Middle East. They accepted slavery as part of everyday life. In fact, only recently, Saudi Arabia, Yemen, Oman, and Mauritana outlawed slavery. In 1981, Maurtania became the last country in the world to abolish slavery. In my study of ancient India, the terms *dasa* and *dasyu* in Vedic literature is translated as 'slave' or 'servant.' Sources such as Arthashastra, Smritis, and Mahabharata show that institutionalized slavery was firmly entrenched in India before the end of the first millennium BCE."

Ahmed raised his hand to get everyone's attention. He quietly added, "I recently became an American citizen. What confused me is that our Founding Fathers of this great nation, while they were writing our Constitution and fighting for our liberty, they owned hundreds of slaves. George Washington, Benjamin Franklin, Thomas Jefferson, James Madison, and Patrick Henry were all slave owners. History books rarely mention these grave injustices. African slaves were counted as property rather than humans. Shops proudly displayed signs that blacks and dogs are not allowed inside. Are we ashamed to accept that our heroes and the icons of our liberty and freedom could participate in these grave injustices to mankind? There is certainly a double standard here. In all fairness, later, the Founding Fathers did support the abolition of slavery."

Everyone was quiet for a moment. Talkative Baijoo was swift to jump into our interesting conversation. He added, "In my first book, *The Journey of an Immigrant: The American Dream*, I wrote about my forefathers from India were lost in a foreign land, Trinidad, with a strange culture, but adaptation was their key to survival. When the British ended slavery in 1833, the freed Africans refused to work in the sugarcane fields any longer. The shrewd British lords formulated a devious plan called the Indian indenture system or another subtle form of slavery. In India, the British ensured that there was massive unemployment, famine, and starvation unto their subjects. The Indians had no choice but to flee from their homeland. Between 1833 and 1920, 3.5 million East Indians were transported to various British colonies. By the way, they brought marijuana for use intended for overcoming long backbreaking hours. Their contracts were for five years with a handsome wage of twelve cents per month plus measly rations. The conquerors ensured that the indentured Indians remain illiterate, but the Indians were a resilient people. They sacrificed their happiness and ensured their children received the highest education on their meager wages. They knew that education held the key from the shackles of slavery. This massive migration resulted in the development of a large Indian diaspora which spread from Africa, Mauritius, Fiji, the Caribbean giving rise to Indo-Caribbean, Indo-Fijian, Indo-Mauritian, and Indo-African populations. Hindu and Muslim marriages were not approved in the colonies, only Christian marriages. Children born in those illegal bonds were deemed illegitimate or not sanctioned by the law. Throughout their vast colonies, the British tried massive conversion to Christianity. They failed miserably with the Indians. The religious data on India Census 2011 showed Hindus were 79.8 percent (966.3 million), Muslims were 14.23 percent (172.2 million), and Christians were only 2.30 percent (8.3 million)."

Anita interrupted Baijoo's long and winding speech. "The British used their colonies as bargaining chips for trade and war. On September 2, 1940, as the Battle of Britain intensified, the United States Secretary of State, Mr. Cordell Hull signaled an agreement to transfer American warships to the Royal Navy. In exchange, the USA was granted land use in the tactical areas in the worldwide British colonies. A lease was granted for ninety-nine years, rent-free. The American leased bases in Trinidad for many years. I was raised in Tobago. My grandfather spoke highly of the numerous Yankee soldiers visiting Tobago. On the island on leave of absence, they would go on spending splurges on wine, women, parties and foods. They loved the island's spicy foods immensely."

She became emotional as she spoke on slavery. "Man's inhumanity to man never ceases to amaze me. True, we are animalistic in our behavior."

Suddenly, Anita and Lisa's eyes traveled in a different direction to a tall handsome soldier neatly dressed in uniform with a bouquet of red roses in his hands. They rushed to greet their guest like a cheetah stalking its prey. My aging heart skipped a beat when I realized that it was Lisa's college sweetheart, Alex. They planted a kiss on both of his cheeks as they escorted him in the direction of our table. My wife introduced him to all our seated guests.

He came and hugged me. Alex smiled and said directly to me, "I am sorry, Father. I have been away for too long. It seems that USA is always at war."

Lisa mentioned that author Baijoo was originally from Trinidad. Alex eyes lit up with interest as he was seated in between Lisa and her husband, Ahmed.

He started at once, "You know that my grandfather served in World War II with the US Navy. He was stationed in Chaguaramas, Trinidad, in the West Indies. He always bragged that Trinidad and Tobago have the best variety of foods in the world. After the war ended, he regularly cooked Trini foods for everyone. Sadly, he died in a car accident last year. Here in Miami, I go to Joy's roti shop and Laloos in Broward County for Trini foods. Their meals are delicious and tasty like my grandfather's cooking. At present, my company was stationed in Homestead Air Base, so we found this restaurant to be a perfect location. My friends have been here on numerous occasions. Anita is a perfect hostess. Her staff is super friendly."

Then he cleverly turned his attention to his childhood sweetheart, Lisa. "My love, how are you? We had lost communications for a few years. I came here many, many times, hoping to see you. My sweetheart, I miss you. I met your mother here. She said you were stationed in the Middle East, helping refugees. My company was stationed in Kuwait, South Korea, Iraq, and Japan. A soldier's journey is not his own reckoning but is dictated by the whims and fantasies of the policies of our politicians. A faithful soldier goes wherever our country needs us, even beyond the call of duty. In Iraqi, children of insurgents planted roadside bombs that killed three of my men. I was wounded in that episode and presumed dead by my company. Friendly Iraqis found me wandering in the desert. I was in the hospital and rehabilitation for six months."

Lisa looked fondly at her former sweetheart with admiration. Ahmed looked at her very confused, after Alex's loving gestures toward his wife. Anita and I stared angrily at our daughter. Lisa abruptly interrupted Alex tender words. "Please stop before you proceed any further with your conversation. This is my husband, Ahmed. We have a son. His name is Akram. We met and were married in Syria. I am sorry."

Alex was visibly shaken by this unexpected news. He managed a half-baked smile but was certainly uncomfortable with his former lover's statement. His self-confidence was lost as his smile disappeared from his face.

He mumbled, "But… but, my love. We promised to wait for each other even to the end of the world."

Lisa was visibly upset at the direction of his conversation and hurriedly excused herself from our table. I decided to follow my daughter. In our small circle of friends, everyone knew that Alex was her childhood friend, high school companion, and constant college mate. They were inseparable. Lisa had stopped at our scenic water fountain and rose garden in front of our restaurant, an ideal place for a troubled soul. This was always her place of solace. The ambiance was very tranquil and serene. Lisa sat crying uncontrollably. Her hands covered her face. I placed my hands gently on my daughter's shoulders.

Without looking, she responded, "Daddy, I knew that you would come looking for me. You have always been my protector and strength. However, I am not your angelic daddy's little girl anymore. Papa, I have made many grave mistakes with my life. My love has always been for Alex. I honestly thought that he was killed by terrorists in Iraq with an improvised explosive device. The media reported his death, but it was fake news. You know, I was frustrated and upset at the tragic news of his demise. Seeing my plight, Krishna told me to accompany him to Syria. There, we saw numerous maiming and deaths of children with these roadside bombs. It brought back unpleasant memories of my love, Alex. These refugee's only crime was simply looking for scraps of food on the streets. Today, when I saw Alex, my heart was lit on fire. All my wonderful and tender memories with him came back to me."

Lisa wiped her bloodshot eyes. She turned toward to me with the utmost sincerity in her heart.

"This was my secret from you. In Syria, when the Russian bombers destroyed our hospital, Ahmed and I were trapped inside a room for many days. It was freezing cold. We cuddled intimately together to survive the ordeal. In my most vulnerable moment, Ahmed made love to me. I guess, I wanted to be loved as a woman again. There was no passion between us but a desperate move to survive this traumatic ordeal. I was pregnant but lost my baby. Today, my heart craved to be in the loving arms of Alex. However, my head is saying to save my marriage with Ahmed for the sake of our son, Akram. Divorce is mainly traumatic on children. My husband hardly ever says that he loves me but his actions tells of his love and commitment to me. Nevertheless, Ahmed is a good, loyal, and a devoted father."

My daughter was confused. My answer to her was simple. "Take time away from your marriage and Alex. Sort out your life. Only you can say whether to follow your heart or keep your family together. You are the master of your destiny. I will support and love you in whatever decision is best for you. Lisa, my love, understand clearly that the decision that you make will affect the lives of your loved ones."

We both sat there briefly without realizing that Alex and Ahmed were nearby, listening to our every word. We were startled by their unexpected presence.

"Dr. Cook, can I speak to your daughter alone, please?" Alex politely interrupted.

I walked a few steps away to give them some privacy but could still overhear their emotional conversation. Ahmed looked at me, very muddled, then suspiciously observed Lisa and Alex in quiet conversation. His ears were tuned into their every word. His wife told Alex, "When you joined the army, I lived with that fear, that dreaded feeling that one day, I will get a call that you were killed in combat. Then one day, the big media outlets showed your company being ambushed in Iraq, and the soldiers' bodies were burned on the streets. I cried for days, thinking you were dead. Alex, I waited and waited for you. I was an emotional wreck. Seeing my agony, Krishna suggested we help the refugees in Syria. I turned my attention with my brother helping the displaced refugees in Syria. There, I met my husband. He loves me, and that is important to me. I am sorry, but our past is only pleasant memories. I admire my husband. I cannot change my journey for nothing."

Alex replied sadly, "I still love you, but I respect that decision. Goodbye."

Alex rushed to the door. Lisa hurried to the bathroom. Ahmed and I stood silently. Her past life was never discussed again.

Enjoy Your Journey

No matter how problematic life's journey develops, never give up. Never stop trying. The only limitations in life journeys are what we place on ourselves. Incurable diseases and emotional distresses, such as divorce, are inevitable dramas of our journey. Do not allow these limitations to keep you in the dark closet of your life. Accept every challenge with a smile, pray and move on.

There was a strong-minded boy whose father was a farmer. He worked diligently to be admitted to the prestigious Oxford University in England. At Oxford, he enjoyed acting, but he could not perform well due to a speaking disorder. He did not have a heroic body or a handsome face like Brad Pitt, but he wanted to prove everyone wrong. Through hard work and determination, he started his own television series, *Mr. Bean*. His legend became one of the most famous international celebrities. Success comes with willpower and working diligently.

Famous movie stars such as Bruce Willis, Julia Roberts, Samuel Jackson, James Earl Jones, and Marilyn Monroe all stammered. Today they are famous. Readers, do not be a living dead to your society, but make a valuable contribution regardless of your limitations. Remember that a vehicle in motion stays in motion. Do not be caught in a doldrum of life but sail bravely into uncharted waters. Do not allow diseases or distress to hinder you from moving and enjoying life. Remember the story about the donkey, man, and the boy in a previous chapter. Enjoy your life. Learn to laugh and cry at your mistakes. Dance through life like no one is watching. Dance like is there no tomorrow. We have no choice in birth and death, so enjoy your journey in life. Mother Teresa pertinently writes about life:

> Life is an opportunity, benefit from it.
> Life is a beauty, admire it.
> Life is a dream, realize it.
> Life is a challenge, meet it.
> Life is a duty, complete it.
> Life is a game, play it.
> Life is a promise, fulfill it.
> Life is a sorrow, overcome it.
> Life is a song, sing it.
> Life is a struggle, accept it.
> Life is a tragedy, confront it.

Life is an adventure, dare it.
Life is luck, make it.
Life is too precious, do not destroy it.
Life is life, fight for it.

Let this book be a tool to inspire your life.